Savage

Bond

ANNE MARSH

Copyright © 2012 Anne Marsh

All rights reserved. No part of this book may be reproduced in any form or by any means without the prior written consent of the author, excepting brief quotes used in reviews.

Cover design by Anne Cain

ISBN-13: 978-0-9854720-1-6

Look for these titles by Anne Marsh

The Fallen

**BOND WITH ME
HIS DARK BOND
SAVAGE BOND**

Hunter's Mate

THE HUNT

Praise for Anne Marsh and her novels

"A master world builder…"
—*Romantic Times*

"*Bond With Me* is a superb romantic urban fantasy."
—Harriet Klausner

"Fans of fallen angels will eat this one up."
—Anna's Book Blog

"The sexy fallen angel is an exciting new addition to the pantheon of paranormal romance heroes, and Anne Marsh adds to that the dark seduction of bonding your soul to obtain your secret desires. You will be seduced along with Nessa by the deliciously sexy Zer, and as seduction turns to love, you will be enraptured by the Fallen."
—Heroes and Heartbreakers

FORWARD

Three thousand years since they rebelled, since they Fell.
The archangel Michael took their wings, took away their ability to feel.
They were exiled to Earth, and now they tempt the human race with a devil's pact of their own: one soul for one favor.
They are now the Fallen angels. Before, bred to be brutal warriors, they fought for the Heavens as part of the Dominion host. They fought. They defended. They did the archangels' bidding. Heavens' enforcers, nothing stood between them and their duty—until a series of savage murders shook the Heavens and the Dominions rose up against the archangel and chose a new side and a new path.
Now, in the year 2090, they fight to survive on Earth. Fight to control an insatiable thirst for human emotions that threatens to turn them into the ultimate monsters when they can no longer control their desire to drink. Fight to find the one thing that could save them.
A soul mate.
Find his one, pre-destined mate and a Fallen warrior finds his one second chance. Loving her would redeem his soul and regain his wings. He would *feel* once he had bound her to him through the bonding ritual. A ritual that tied their souls together forever. A ritual that marked both the warrior and his woman body and soul. Lose her, however, and he was condemned to live forever without souls or wings. She was his one hope—and his ultimate weakness. She was the last chance for his dying race.

CHAPTER ONE

She was dying. As the chopper banked hard right, Ria Morgan's stomach decided it was a good time to remind her of what she'd had for lunch four hours earlier. The sandwich and greasy fries threatened to make a return trip up her throat despite her best attempts to swallow. Flying was for the birds. And maybe, once upon a time, for the Fallen angels.

Not that the Fallen were fairytale material. That kind of sensuality scared her. Big and hard and edgy, the Fallen were sexy as hell, but she was smart enough to know she didn't want to take all that on. They were beautiful to watch, the way a king cobra or a panther was, but she wasn't getting in a room with one. Closest she got to that sort of beast was at the zoo— with two inches of shatter-proof, bullet-proof glass between herself and the animals.

"You're no good at this flying shit," Lieutenant Jane Reece observed cheerfully, stretching out her booted feet like her ass was parked in her favorite Barcalounger and not five thousand feet in the air. As the pilot did another hard right to avoid the latest mountain ridge springing up in front of the windshield, Reece readjusted the muzzle of the Vektor. Anyone came at them, Reece here had Ria's back. Trouble wasn't expected, but the Fallen were full of surprises, so MVD, M City's paranormal policing unit, wasn't taking chances. The good lieutenant had orders to shoot on sight.

"No good at all," she agreed shortly. Her toes tingled in her sneakers, a prickly connection to the vibrations shaking the chopper's floor.

"Bet you don't like heights, either," Reece suggested. "Explains how you pulled this job. Got the short end of the straw, Morgan?"

Ria got her arms up and braced, pointing the camera down at the target. What she needed here was a tripod, but she'd be making do instead. "Something like that."

She'd spent years learning to read the images she shot for hidden messages. A hangar's size advertised the number of troops that could be concealed inside those four walls. Anything the lens picked up was just one more tip off, broadcasting enemy movements. From the chopper, she had a bird's eye view of just how big the arteries available were for moving troops. She was damned good at reading those signs.

Even if she was usually reading those signs from her office, her ass parked in a desk chair rather than strapped into a jump seat.

Movement unfolded beneath the chopper and she swung the lens around to follow. Vehicles moving over land always left some sort of mark behind — wheel marks, tracks, ruts. The size, shape, and length of vehicles were all there in those distinguishing marks. She couldn't tell yet what was moving beneath her, but something was definitely happening here, where there should have been nothing at all—and she was getting to the bottom of it.

The chopper hit a draft and bucked, and Ria swallowed hard, the lens losing whatever it was she had been tracking. Damn it.

She and heights had the kind of love-hate relationship usually found between brothers and sisters. Angle was good for her shots, but vertigo hit her hard as her brain took in the height. The sheer space between herself and safety made her dizzy, the ground falling away as the chopper ate up the air. She sucked in a breath. *Inhale. Exhale. Focus.* The world on the ground jumped into sharp focus as she zoomed in. The movement she'd spotted wasn't unfriendly, just an animal. Nothing interesting.

She'd been cold moments ago, but now she was burning up, desperate to escape the choking confines of the flight suit. She wasn't in danger, she reminded herself. She just felt like she was, her mind's convenient little mental trick to get her feet back on the ground where her feet belonged. Where she was *safe*.

She knew these feelings. Wait it out, she reminded herself. Just a handful of minutes—two or three—and she'd be okay again. The panic would tuck itself back into the dark corner of her psyche where the fear lurked. Everything would be fine.

Until the next time.

Each time, she hoped the panic attack was the last one, because she had a job to do and the panic was a barrier that got harder and harder to overcome. Each time, she'd been wrong. She'd avoided planes and flying for years, until MVD had forced her ass up into the air.

Ria might work for MVD, but she wasn't an agent. The covert stuff made her nervous, made her want to throw up from the adrenaline dancing its way through her nervous system. She was strictly backroom and support. She watched, she sent the little unmanned drone winging through the air and over Fallen territory to do the snap-and-click, and she processed the images the drone sent back electronically.

All from the peace and quiet of her office chair. Hum of the servers and the bank of screens in front of her. She was damned good at her job.

She wasn't supposed to be *here* however.

This was no UAV. She wasn't piloting an unmanned aerial drone, driving the little craft through a low altitude sneak in the silent battle between the Fallen and MVD.

No, this was an actual, real life, honest-to-God plane with an engine and a human pilot and five thousand feet of empty space between her feet and the cold, hard ground.

Sure, she'd done six weeks of boot camp for MVD, gritting her teeth through the runs and the sit-ups, the survival training and the arms drills, but she'd done *that* so she could get her hands on their hardware. MVD had the most powerful, most cutting-edge software and hardware of any human organization she'd ever interviewed with. Or hacked her way into. The lure of those bits was powerful, plus the digital world just made sense. Programming was pure logic and she loved it. All cause and effect. If. Then. Neat little branches and subroutines. Predictable, if you could wrap your mind around the code base. And she could.

So it still didn't answer the question of: *why*?

UAVs reacted poorly to weather and there was weather rolling through the Preserves right now. Whatever MVD thought they'd seen, they wanted their second look right now and they weren't waiting for that weather to clear. She was a Combat Systems Officer, her CO had pointed out dryly when she objected to the reassignment, and that meant she was fully qualified for the job at hand. Not to mention she was the *only* CSO available.

And that was just the story of her life, wasn't it? She was always last choice. Never the first. She'd been the only photographer available when word came in that the unmanned drones weren't cutting it and the higher ups wanted to send in a human team. Rain had screwed the cameras to hell and back, but not before the last set of images came back, hinting at unusual movement out here in the Preserves.

"You think we're going to find us any?" The good lieutenant's finger stroked the trigger of the Vektor.

"There aren't supposed to be any angels out here." *Supposed to be* being the key phrase here. There was no denying the rumors about winged angels being spotted flying over M City and in and out of the Preserves. Hence her presence here on the plane, because she got the fun job of confirming or denying those rumors. The Preserves were supposed to be a prison for the Fallen who couldn't keep it together any longer—not a launching pad.

"Yeah." Lieutenant Reece patted the Vektor's barrel as her eyes sifted through the shadows on the ground. The lieutenant was looking for trouble, too. "But if there were, we'd be ready. I'd like to take a shot at them."

The pilot came on the headset. "I'm dropping down to angels two. Get you a good look at our hot spot." The flight plan called for a close-up up on the area where MVD had been getting some disturbing intel. So far, all they had were high-aerial satellite shots, which meant not enough detail. To get the close-ups, her ass was out here on a plane.

In and out.

Something was going down, but fucking Fallen angels hadn't shared the 4-1-1. All stonewall and "No, ma'am, nothing happening here."

Air slammed into the chopper as Lieutenant Reece forced the side door open. Ria hated flying, hated this part of the job, but the paralyzing fear wasn't lifting until her feet were back on the ground, so she'd do her job here and then she'd go home.

Which was more than the occupants of the Preserves would be doing anytime soon.

The Preserves were no rest home, that was for damn sure. She wasn't sure how or if the bastard angels could be killed, but this was where the worst of the lot went to wait out their days when their own kind finally decided they were too dangerous to run around unchecked. Just a fancier way of saying *prison*, because that's what the Preserves were. And, if the bad apples of the Fallen world had found themselves a revolving door from their prison, the consequences wouldn't be pretty for M City.

She hated that she was afraid, hated the way fear tied her gut up in knots. She couldn't let that fear stop her, however. She was the best photographer MVD had.

There. Movement again beneath the bird on the ground. "Take us down closer," she commed. She needed a better shot—this was big. Bigger than she'd suspected was possible.

Surrounded by rocky canyons, an unfamiliar Fallen angel stood in the center of the others like he was the mother lode of all things magical. When she adjusted the zoom, using the camera's lens to get up close and personal, she could see his lips moving. And, with each word he pronounced, new marks appeared on the bared backs of the Fallen angels surrounding him. The marks glowed red in the slowly gathering twilight, as if they had some kind of life of their own.

One minute and five hundred feet later, she knew the truth. The speaker shut his yap and his companions hit the ground, as if their legs were just done holding them up. Even from her bird's eye view perch in the sky, the screaming came through loud and clear, punctuating the crimson lace of bloody droplets hanging from the surrounding trees. Red wings tore through the skin of their backs.

"Fallen don't have wings, right?"

Lieutenant Reece shook her head. "Never have had yet. Supposed to be part and parcel of that divine punishment package they've got going on. No wings. No soul. No Heavens."

"Then something's changed." Ria didn't move the camera from the scene unfolding in the clearing below, kept her finger working the shutter. Whatever was happening down there looked damned close to some sort of ritual.

"Well, shit." Reece's curse summed it up well as far as Ria was concerned.

"Yeah." Unless she was mistaken, she'd just shot a one-two-three tutorial for making monsters.

Those Fallen bastards had wings. They weren't supposed to be able to fly. That was the deal as she'd heard it. Three thousand years ago, the archangel Michael had exiled his Dominion warriors from the Heavens for staging a rebellion. He'd ripped their wings off and thrown them down to Earth. Not like she appreciated her home being used as the celestial equivalent of a penal colony, but truth was truth. The Dominions had become the Fallen and *none* of them could fly.

Except these Fallen clearly could.

One of the newly winged creatures soared up through the air. Her camera clicked instinctively, but her mind was screaming *Wrong*.

She wasn't second-guessing this and the intel couldn't wait. As soon as the pilot had opened up a line, she commed back to M City. MVD needed to hear this.

Her boss's voice came in loud and clear— and filled with annoyance: "This channel is not secure," he snapped. "Next time, wait until you're secure before you call in."

Next time? "This can't wait," she argued. "I'm sending pics," she said, starting the upload. Connection was poor and it would take time to move those images over, but she wanted eyes on this.

"Roger that." Before her boss could say more, the chopper jerked sharply left.

"We've got bogeys." The pilot cursed. "Not sure who or what, but definitely hostile."

Reece looked out the open door and cursed again. "Bastards definitely have themselves some wings."

More curses came from the pilot's seat, as the man got on the headset back to base, his fingers racing to find a secured channel. Reece shot her a glance. "Hold tight," she ordered and then she put the Vektor to work, firing round after round out the open door.

Ria knew the chopper wasn't built to sustain this kind of attack. There had to be thirty winged angels all slamming bodily into the chopper and already the bird veered hard left with the first hit. As an angel banked and came about for a second pass, the glowing red runes on its back lit up the sky. The next hit jarred her teeth, the vibrations tearing through her body.

How long could they take this kind of damage?

"Suit up." Reece didn't take her eyes off the fight unfolding outside the chopper, jerking her chin towards the chutes hanging from the webbing. Fingers trembling, Ria pulled on the chute.

"We've got a hard landing at best," Reece continued. Worst was crash, but the other woman didn't waste breath pointing out the obvious.

MVD had set Ria up with a Black Hawk helicopter for today's field trip. The chopper could fly at low altitude, which meant she could get her shots. Unfortunately, at the end of the day, the chopper was still just a machine. The pilot was maneuvering them through the Preserves' rocky canyons, but the bird was barely making those turns, the blades fighting for lift.

The winged angels *that weren't supposed to exist* descended towards the chopper. The pilot dropped the bird even lower to evade, but he couldn't avoid the powerful downward push of air from all those alien wings. The chopper wasn't built for bat-turns, the blades whining as the pilot forced the bird to turn tight and hard. The one-eighty heading change slammed Ria against the side, her hands instinctively cradling the camera.

The bird whipped erratically as the pilot shot out of the last canyon and abandoned low-and-evasive for climbing fast and hard.

The sun was dropping steadily beneath the horizon, the light going quick. Wind had picked up on the ground, too, so between the sunset and the wind, they were going to have brown-out conditions on the ground. If they even *made* it to the ground in one piece.

"Shit." The lieutenant cursed as she squeezed off rounds. The deafening roar of the Vektor bounced off the sides of the chopper.

"Secure the card, Morgan. Do it."

Between the devil and the deep blue. Before she could second guess herself, Ria popped the memory card out of the camera, unzipping the front of her flight suit as she considered her options. Then slid the card into her bra cup. The cold, hard poke of plastic was a wake-up call she could have done without.

The chopper shuddered, jerking hard as something heavy slammed into the tail.

"Check six," Reece growled. "We've got to hurry."

The pilot cursed. "Roger that."

He'd got them up to ten thousand feet now, which meant engine power was dropping off. Fast. Their ride was meant for recon, not high altitude. Reaching around her, Reece released the protective webbing on the west bay door. "I'll lay down cover on the east side. You're out the side. Count fifteen and pull the handle."

"We can go higher, fly out of this." Ria stared at Reece, willing the other woman to agree with her. She couldn't jump. No way.

"No." Lieutenant Reece kept it short and sweet, fingers unhooking Ria's protective harness from the side of the chopper. *Oh, God.* "Get your ass into that bay. On my count, you jump. Feet down. Arms in. Clear the plane, count it down to forty and then I pull the cord. And, Morgan?"

"Yeah?"

"You don't jump, I push."

"Do it quick," she said and Reece nodded. The bird jerked hard again and she steeled herself for the jump. Because it was jump or die and she wasn't ready to die.

Vkhin's headset crackled, coming alive, as the slim figure ejected in slow motion from the open chopper bay. Ten thousand feet up, but his view from the helo was still ringside. The gloved hand hitting the small of the jumper's back had him growling. That hand had touched *her*. He knew the body falling free of the chopper. Not as well as he wanted, but he'd been watching her for the last month and Fallen intel said she'd gone up in the plane. One pilot. One ride-along MVD agent. And Ria Morgan.

Ria's body cleared the chopper and he fought his instinctive reaction. That bird was going down and he didn't want her anywhere near the wreck. He'd warned Zer and the other Fallen that MVD was getting too bold, making moves that would take the human police division right into Fallen territory. Looked like he was going to have the proof he needed. Unfortunately, his professional responsibilities here were at war with something more feral. Possessive. Ria Morgan was *his*.

She might be a card-carrying member of MVD and an enemy hostile in *his* territory, but he wanted her. A rogue dropped away from others going after the chopper, circling back around the protective fire Ria's human companion was laying down. The gunner laid in counter-fire and the rogue dropped. If Ria was lucky and the other MVD agent was a good shot, Ria just might make it to the ground.

Good. He commed in on his headset. "I've got a visual. One jumper. Rest of the crew is staying put. I'm going closer."

Punching in his new coordinates, he drove the helo towards the chopper without waiting for confirmation from base.

His response to Ria was irrational. She was a backroom operative, a desk jockey. Smart as a whip—he wouldn't make the mistake of underestimating her brain—but she pulled her nine-to-five and left the dirty stuff to MVD's field agents. She went into that office building every morning, real punctual. She stopped briefly to pick up a mocha—guilty weakness—and a doughnut, while he knew the same untouched energy bar banged around in the bottom of her over-sized purse every morning. She favored slim pencil skirts and buttoned up white blouses in real soft syn-cotton that clung to her breasts beneath the oversized cardigans she wrapped around herself because she was always cold. A sexy skirt and blouse like that just begged for four-inch heels, but, no, she paired the ensemble with an endless series of black ballerina flats. That mismatch intrigued him. Because, if she wore the flats because they were comfortable or she enjoyed them, what did that say about her taste in skirts? Those skirts cupped her ass, were made from soft fabrics that rubbed against her skin with every step she took, slid temptingly upward when she sat down at that desk of hers, crossed her legs, and leaned forward, going for the joystick controlling her drone. Those skirts were a sensual treat.

He just wanted to know who she was treating.

He, on the other hand, was a warrior, a hand-to-hand fighter who'd climbed into far too many trenches and done whatever killing needed to be done. He didn't need to be jonesing after a woman who clearly not only didn't know the meaning of down and dirty, but had no intention of ever leaving the pristine confines of her office. He respected MVD's field agents because those men and women put it on the line every day. Every weapon they strapped on, every fight they broke up or started—those were acts he could respect. Coffee and a doughnut were a whole different world.

So he shouldn't have wanted to slide the zipper on her skirt down, peel the soft fabric away from her even softer skin and spread her wide for his tongue. She wasn't his type. She was human. And she was off-limits.

Nevertheless, he couldn't stop watching her. He didn't think she knew he was there, or at least not that he was there for her. She had eyes and ears everywhere, because she was MVD's agent and he was one of Zer's lieutenants and a formidable player in the game the Fallen were playing. Not watching him would have been a mistake and he didn't think Ria Morgan made too many of those. He shouldn't have wondered, though, what it would take to coax her outside of her nice, safe office. What it would take to make her see *him* and not another target for her lenses and cameras. But he kept coming back, circling around her building and going places he knew she was watching because his own techs warned him her drones were overhead, unseen but tracking him through the sky.

Right now, things were game over for Ria Morgan.

Her face on his handheld haunted him and it shouldn't have. Ria Morgan had the face of an angel and Vkhin had seen more than his share. Her face wasn't a bold face. Chin tilted down, she looked up into the photographer's camera with a sexy pout. He'd have bet the wings he no longer had that the sexiness was accidental on her part. She was just looking when she was told to smile for the camera and sure, on the surface of things, she was fairly Plain Jane with shoulder-length brown hair. Pretty, but not beautiful by human standards. That hair of hers, however, hid shades of honey and her hazel eyes were ringed with just a hint of green. She was a surprise package just waiting to be unwrapped.

And it got harder every day—and night—not to unwrap Ria Morgan.

Running MVD's drone program gave her that creamy skin because she spent all that time indoors and not out, but there was a spray of freckles that teased him something bad. He wanted to follow that trail down, from her ear, over her collarbone; to see if, when he unwrapped her, laid her bare, she was hiding freckles from him elsewhere. That beautiful skin of hers would be sensitive. She had no idea how long he'd been watching her watch him, but, God help him, just the sight of the drones flying overhead got him hard now.

But at least the drones kept her safe inside where she wasn't going to end up hurt or worse. She needed to be kept safe from males like him. He smiled fiercely, a mere baring of his teeth. He wanted to *hunt* her, force her out of her shadows and into his world where he could have her.

Unfortunately, she was *here*, flying over the Preserves and shooting pics. It had to be something really good. Something tantalizing enough to pull her out of her nice, safe box and take the chance. Which meant it was something that could get her killed.

He'd be happy to teach her all about action and reaction and what happened when she took on the big boys. This wasn't a game. She'd invaded. He'd defend. For one long moment, he let himself imagine taking Ria Morgan into his bed, stripping away all those clothes and the control she wrapped around herself. His mouth taking her as he dragged his tongue through her soaked folds. *No.* He forced his mind away from the erotic fantasy. She was pure weakness. His weakness.

Falling through the empty air, she looked impossibly fragile. Human. Her slim dark shape hurtled towards the ground, trailing a line from the chopper to her chute. One of her human companions would pull her chute for her. Good. He was betting jumping wasn't a skill she'd practiced real recent.

The Fallen handling comm duties pulled his attention back. "Negative that. Stay airborne."

Like hell he would. Almost out of fuel, he could turn around and head back—or he could put the helo down, quick and hard. Take his chances inside the Preserves. Go after Ria Morgan.

Yeah. That last option appealed.

"No." The jump line jerked and the chute shot open, pulling Ria up and back for a long moment before the wind caught her. She was drifting east, away from the wall. Vkhin adjusted his course. "I'm out. I'm setting the helo down."

The pithy curse on the other end pretty much summed up the FUBAR nature of this assignment. "You want backup?"

Because of the heavily warded walls, only a Fallen with wings or a helo could make it in and out of the Preserves. Out of fuel, he'd need a pick up or he'd be trapped inside the Preserves. "Not yet. I'm going to need a pick up."

"Roger that."

He sent the helo shooting over the canopy. Just west of him, MVD's chopper put up a valiant battle, the sharp retort of the Vektor chewing up the airspace. Some hits, too, but the only way to kill a former angel—Fallen or rogue—was to take the head off. Whatever damage the chopper's human crew was inflicting was only temporary.

The moment MVD's bird had crossed into the Preserves' air space, the intrusion had triggered a warning. Vkhin's mission here was crystal clear. Hunt down the chopper violating the Preserves' airspace. Destroy said chopper and take the humans out of the equation.

Of course, right now it looked like the rogues with wings were going to take care of the chopper for him. The rotor blade cracked as a rogue slammed into it. That hit was a suicide mission, yeah, but effective. The tail rotor failed as the rogue's weight blocked the blades and the chopper yawed hard right. The chopper had been pushing hard to gain altitude, and now the failure sent it spinning. Even at this distance, Vkhin could clearly hear the whine of the engine cutting out. Less than a minute later, the other aircraft was going down in a ball of fire. Coming down near him. He moved out, towards the dark column of smoke.

The chute disappeared beneath the canopy slightly east of the earth-bound chopper. He wanted to go straight to her, but he still had responsibilities. Logic dictated he check out the crash site first. He needed to verify that there were no other survivors—and that she'd left nothing incriminating behind her.

Damn it. He hit the throttle hard, gunning for the crash site. He got there first. Not the rogues who were going to be hunting her sweet little ass. Tree canopy ripped greedily at the belly of the stealth helo as he drove the small craft forward.

What did she think would happen when a manned MVD spy plane disappeared inside the Preserves? MVD couldn't cop openly to the mission, not without some serious proof of wrongdoing, which meant she had to know what she was doing now. That it was all on the line, because the only way she got out now was on her own or with a miracle. She couldn't be so fucking blind that she didn't know that. Maybe MVD would try to send a rescue mission for her. It was possible. His teeth clenched together. They could try. Only way she got out of here now was with him.

He was going to make that perfectly clear when he got his hands on her.

He only hoped she was ready for him.

He put the helo down hard, barely registering the jolt before he was out. Burning pieces of chopper rained down lazily around him, feeding the cold, lethal rage building inside him.

The comm barked back to life. "Are you in position for a look-see?"

"I've got visual on the crash site." He reconned the crash site rapidly, striding over to the smoking wreckage. The pilot had died in his seat, still webbed in. Equally clearly, the Vektor's owner had got out the door, but whether or not she had had enough altitude to deploy her chute was unknown. She was low enough to have hit the ground hard. Neither of them were supposed to be here. Both were threats to his kind.

As were the rogues circling back for a second round.

He hit the comm fast. "I've got incoming. I need to get in and get out. One dead human—two bail outs. Ria Morgan and a second MVD agent. Jumps were roughly ten minutes apart, so they didn't stick together."

A rough curse broke the silence on other end and then there was a pause with a whole lot of what-ifing going on in the background. "We've got a complication. We're tracking an outbound call from that chopper. Right before the pilot sent out his distress call, someone on board uploaded pictures."

Fuck. What had she seen? His jaw tightened. Because of course she'd seen something she shouldn't have. That was the whole reason for MVD to infiltrate. "What did she get?"

There was a brief pause and click of keys as the other Fallen worked the keyboard. "Sender went wireless and didn't bother with protection. Must have figured the airspace was pretty secure. I hijacked the session as it went outbound, so MVD's pretty much got nothing. Just the file headers."

"So MVD knows there's a flag on the play and the chopper caught something, but they don't know what."

"Check the chopper, then find the jumper, get the vidstick if she still has it and destroy it. Header file tells MVD what she had were images and gives them the size, but nothing too useful. They're going to need the source for that."

No word on getting his ass out of the Preserves but he hadn't expected it. If there was a way to do it and he was still sane, he knew Zer would do what he could. Otherwise, Zer was right where he needed to be. All locked up, good and tight.

"Why do her damned pictures matter so much?" Vkhin asked. He was already covering his tracks, about to move out, when the glint of metal caught his eye. Reaching out, he snagged a gold bracelet from the wreck. The fragile links had caught on the doorframe. The metal still carried her scent, but the skin warmth was gone from the thin metal already. Soon, the bracelet would be nothing more than a handful of bent links.

There was a pause on the other end of the comm and then Zer got on the line.

"We've already got a problem with rogues regaining their wings. Those wings are a get-out-of-jail-free card we can't afford. Photog got close-ups of the runes used to wing up the latest lot of rogues."

"You think someone else can recreate the process based on her pics?"

There was a pause and then, "I'm not taking that chance," Zer said grimly.

"We won't know until we see what she got. Track her. Bring her back to the base."

Vkhin didn't say no when Zer asked for something, which meant Zer didn't ask unless he needed the work done.

Hesitation colored the other Fallen's voice. "Doesn't have to be you who goes in."

"Someone goes. And I'm already here." He was okay with ending up dead. Hell, ending up dead was a best case scenario for him. Almost as good was staying put inside the Preserves. All he lived for now was the fight. Weapons were good. Nothing like pitting his blade against another's, the quick, determined slash of steel through skin and the sensation of flesh giving. Parting. Opening up for him the way nothing else did now. That was all good.

If he didn't make it back, that was good, too.

There was a pause and then his comm set came alive again, Zer's voice coming over the open line. His sire sounded pissed off. And accepting. Nothing new there. Life was a bitch and this was war. They both knew that battles demanded sacrifices. No problem. He'd be Fate's bitch today.

"No matter what it takes. Offer to bond with her. See what she wants." Bonding would make things simpler, because it would give Vkhin a direct in to her head. She'd be *his* to command.

On the other hand, he'd owe her one.

"I'll get the pics," he snarled. He didn't do bonds anymore. Not after the disaster he'd made of his last bond.

"Be careful," Zer said finally. "And that's an order, Vkhin. We're not the only ones after her. We're seeing rogue movement everywhere. They're fanning out, searching for her. It won't be long before they pick up her trail."

Ria Morgan wasn't a foot soldier. The odds of her having worked in the field, behind enemy lines, were slim to none and yet now she was the target of a massive manhunt. She was vulnerable and he didn't like that.

He pulled a blade.

Moving silently, he slipped slowly back into the darkest shadows wrapped around the crash site and the rogues' little meet-and-greet. He recognized the sound of the bastards' wings. Logically, he knew he should care. The rogues weren't supposed to have wings. That they did was a secret the Fallen had carefully guarded from the humans. Unfortunately, the soul thirst ruled him almost 24/7 now and all he truly cared about was that another, larger predator had made moves on his territory.

Not, he thought, savoring the rare glimmer of his long-gone humanity, that he hadn't been possessive before the soul thirst had got so bad. He'd been a fuck-up even before he'd come here.

Glancing over his shoulder, he glided over the hard ground, erasing his backtrail as he moved. He didn't want to be found. Couldn't risk further exposure because the Preserves were a prison for the most bestial of his kind and, like beasts, they'd turn on him and hunt him if he became too great a threat.

Still, leaving *her* here wasn't right. He might be little better than an animal now, but there was still something left that he could do before life finished kicking his ass and finished him.

Ria's face flashed through his memory. He was already shifting through the variables as he kicked the stealth helo into overdrive.

The angle of the wind and her chute limited her possible landing sites. He'd find her and he'd take what he need.

She didn't stand a chance.

CHAPTER TWO

Oh, God. She didn't stand a chance. The chute deployed with a hard snap, a short, brutal jolt that shoved Ria's feet upward into her spine and her jaw. Worse, when her head jerked backwards, she could see the rogues circling the wounded chopper like a pack of vultures. Minutes latter, the shockwave of the chopper going down tore through her.

Maybe they jumped, too. Maybe, they're coming down right behind me. She forced her eyes open against the sting of angry tears, made her numb fingers curl around the toggles. She couldn't think about the pilot. Or Jane Reece. She had less than two thousand feet to grieve and then she needed to focus on surviving. If the pilot and Lieutenant Reece were going to trade their lives for her pictures, she got those pictures out. No matter what.

She looked up before she could stop herself.

The sky immediately overhead was empty.

Maybe, her companions had had time to jump, too. They'd need five hundred feet minimum to make a landing. Still, she couldn't help looking back as the ground rushed up to meet her. The sky above remained stubbornly empty except for the ever-expanding smear of black smoke.

Okay. She stretched her fingers on the chute's toggles. She'd take the empty sky as a heads-up to focus on her future—which was going to be real short if she didn't keep her hands on the toggles and steer through the canopy. Still, memories of Jane Reece's face kept sneaking through her head, the resigned look on the other woman's face as she got Ria out the door and to safety.

No one deserved to die like that.

Night was coming fast, hiding a multitude of sins. Still, the sky was light enough to see the oily black smoke of the downed chopper punching up from the ground, a here-I-am beacon she couldn't afford. To the west, rogues still circled in the sky. Those large, bestial wings chewed up the air, stroking up and down as they hunted her. They were coming for her. Soon. She knew it, bone deep.

She was prey.

She hit the ground every bit as hard as she could, tucking and rolling. For a moment, the world turned upside down, jolting, as she plowed into the half-frozen ground. *You can do this.* She didn't have a choice. Slapping the pockets of her jumpsuit, she came up with the utility knife and sliced the chute's lines. No human had mapped the Preserves, unless you counted century-old Soviet work that was little more than a blank outline overlaid on vast, empty space. Everyone knew where the borders were—but no one knew quite what to expect inside them. Too bad she was more color-inside-the-lines than intrepid explorer. What she wanted here was a GPS unit. Hell, she'd take an old-fashioned compass.

She needed an exit route. Fast.

She also needed a back up detail, stat, but somehow she knew even a full MVD riot battalion wouldn't be enough to protect her from the rogue Fallen hunting her. That had been an organized strike. The recon chopper had been deliberately attacked, forced down, and the rogue incoming had to have seen her chute out. Maybe, Reece's fire had deterred them or maybe they'd just been too busy taking down the chopper to pursue immediately, but Ria was a sitting duck on the ground. She didn't have the military training to hide from her pursuers, so no shit they could let her land then pick her off at their convenience.

Cover and conceal.

Pinpoint the hostiles.

Phrases from the training manual she'd never expected to need flashed through her head. Color her cynical, but she wasn't expecting the locals to be in a friendly mood. The Fallen hadn't locked their brethren up for being boy scouts.

She broke away from the chute, fighting back panic. Two minutes. She'd give herself two minutes on the ground to organize, because she had to do this logically and because she didn't want to die. There was a survival kit in her pack, so chalk one up in the plus column. She had the 9 MM service pistol all MVD operatives carried, but a limited amount of ammo.

She needed a plan.

And she needed to get moving.

Signaling a rescue chopper was unlikely, especially beneath the tree cover, so her best option was to hike out. They'd been maybe fifteen miles from border when they went down.

MVD would send a rescue chopper.

Wouldn't they?

"No doubting," she muttered to herself and got going.

Twenty minutes into her hike, she knew she had someone on her trail. No way her team had dropped in a rescue party that fast, which meant her company had come from inside the Preserves. And she wasn't counting on any friendlies here.

She ran like she had demons from hell chasing her ass—which was actually a possibility—riding the adrenaline rush as she pushed back the panic and the fear. Foot up. Foot down. She watched her path because the ground wasn't level and she couldn't afford to fall now. Each breath she took was a rough, hoarse saw of sound. She figured she'd either pass out or have to stop to puke because right now nausea and exhaustion were winning this battle. On the other hand, maybe she'd make the distance. It was possible. Marathoners did it, right?

Her flight suit was thick and water-resistant, but, since she hadn't planned to go up at all, all she had on underneath was a lacy bra and panty set and a borrowed t-shirt. Her sneakers had been soaked through since her first step on the ground. At least she was *on* the ground, she reminded herself. That was a good thing. She shuddered and that was all it took to buy the farm. Her feet went out from underneath her as she slipped on the rain-slick ground.

"Damn it," she muttered, hitting the ground hard.

"Language," a harsh voice growled from the shadows behind her.

Fear stole her breath. She scooted backwards on her hands and backside. The retreat wasn't elegant and she didn't care. A primitive flight response shrieked through her. Go, go, go. Whoever—whatever—was in the shadows was going to hurt her. She hated the little whimper she couldn't quite bite back. She didn't want to be scared, but she never got better. A familiar face popped into her head, head shaking as he watched the mess she was making of this job. Daddy had been right. She'd never be strong enough or good enough to handle this job.

"Go away," she choked out, because she was all about wishful thinking, wasn't she? She'd hoped she could handle a simple fly-over but now here she was, stranded on the ground, with no real idea of what to do next or how to handle the shit that was headed her way. The male in the shadows moved and she fought the urge to curl up in a ball and just wait for whatever hurt he wanted to hand out.

A hand came towards her. Large and too strong, that hand ended in capable, blunt fingers. The skin was golden-brown, cut up badly with small scars and paler marks. He'd scraped a wrist coming after her and the blood from that torn skin marked the back of his hand. That was the hand of a fighter and a male who used those hands ruthlessly. His hands weren't pretty, so she certainly didn't want to see the rest of him.

"Ria Morgan," the voice continued and the rest of the man slid out of the shadows and came for her. Too big and large. Too fast. No way he was human. She got up on her hands and knees, finding her feet. She didn't care which direction she went. As long as that direction was *away*, she was good with the choice. He knew who she was. Tears she couldn't stop leaked from her eyes.

"No," she said. He knew who she was and she knew he wasn't human. Which meant he'd come here looking for her and no way she wanted to know what he wanted from her. She got upright and tried to run.

He got an arm around her waist and she was hauled up against a large, hard, hot body, her legs kicking uselessly. That heat was a shock. "What kind of trouble have you found for yourself, Ria?"

"Let me go." As threats went, it was a weak one. His harsh laugh told her he knew that, too.

"Finders keepers, isn't that what you humans say? I've found you, Ria Morgan. Now, I'm keeping you."

"No," she protested automatically. Legs trembling, recognition hit her. That big, dark shadow had spelled trouble from the first. Vkhin. Lieutenant and right-hand of the leader of the Fallen. His harsh face was all hard lines and planes, those dark eyes staring relentlessly out of his face at her, a predator watching his prey. Watching *her*.

She knew him. Oh, God, she *knew* him. She'd spent weeks tracking his movements around M City. Watching him go about his day-in-day-out, taking care of business for the Fallen. He'd killed ruthlessly, but his targets had been other paranormals and MVD didn't interfere with those kinds of internal politics. He was an enforcer and the paranormals who broke his rules died hard and quick, the memories making her stomach heave. He was examining her with those cold, black eyes of his and she hoped to God she wasn't on his to do list for today.

But he hadn't let go of her and she wasn't stupid.

"You have something of ours, something I want and you're going to give it to me." The wave of sexual heat washing over her was wrong. She shouldn't have been aroused by his reluctant touch. Most of the Fallen had sex with their human groupies, some kind of sexual bonding and emotional vampirism. Those women hadn't looked like they minded. At all. She couldn't imagine doing the acts they'd done with those hard-bodied, empty-eyed males.

Or so she'd told herself. She didn't want *that*. She didn't want him.

But she'd watched. Over and over. And he'd never touched a woman, never bent that dark head of his to another woman's throat and pressed his kisses against her skin. And she'd wondered why. Why was he different from the rest of *them*?

"Ria." He crooned her name, the word a dark promise against her ear. She stopped fighting because there was no point. He was bigger, stronger—and some part of her felt safe when he held her. She knew he didn't want to hold her, not like a lover would. This was simply the easiest way for him to pin her.

He knew her name. The thrill of fear that rushed through her made her stomach and knees go weak. The prickly awareness was painfully close to sexual arousal, the nerve endings in her body coming to screaming awareness.

"You need my help, sweetheart."

"Let me go," she said, "and I'll consider it."

To her surprise, he let her go, but kept that loose grasp on her wrist, turning her to face him when she moved away. As if she could somehow get enough space between them for a head start.

"This is your idea of helping?"

He let go. "Don't run," he warned.

"Or?" she asked bitterly. She wrapped a hand around her wrist, stroking her thumb over the veins where her pulse beat betrayingly. God, she was tired of being afraid all the time. Tired of fearing fear itself.

"I can chase you again." His dark growl of a voice was rough. Honest. "Maybe you'd like that."

His hand returned, wrapping around her wrist, his thumb replacing hers, stroking over her pulse point. That unexpected touch was strangely calming, anchoring her. What he was doing, that simple little connection, shouldn't have felt so good. She should have been able to do this for herself. By herself.

"Are you hurt?" he asked, but he didn't let go.

Instead, he eyed her, clearly giving her the once over for injuries. That slow, methodical search had her blood heating.

She shook her head. "I'm fine." *Maybe.*

"Good," he growled, "because my number one priority here is getting your ass back over the wall, not kissing boo-boos."

"No," she said coolly. Her pulse was slowing back down, her heartbeat no longer pounding painfully in her ears. He didn't let go of her wrist, just tugged her that little bit closer. She needed more than eighteen inches between her and six and a half feet of pure temptation. "I landed just fine."

He nodded. "That makes the evac easier."

She stared at him curiously. "You're really here to get me out?" He didn't look like standard search-and-rescue. But she liked the idea, liked the fantasy of tossing all her problems onto those broad shoulders and holding on while he did the heavy lifting.

That was just fantasy, though. Reality was, she'd stood on her own two feet before. She'd do it again this time.

And even as she told herself to just step away, she was stepping closer. He was smoke and mirrors, an illusive promise of safety. He wasn't the real deal. Couldn't possibly save her from the nightmares tearing up the Preserves.

Because, at heart, he was one of them.

His next words just proved it.

"I'm getting you out of here," he said, "just as soon as you hand over the vidstick."

Well, that just sucked. She tugged her wrist and he gave it back to her, his fingers sliding against hers as he backed it up a step.

"What vidstick?" she asked, playing for time. She knew damned well what he meant, but admitting that truth seemed unwise. Single female alone in a deserted place with a supernaturally powerful male? Yeah. Classic recipe for disaster.

"Ria." He sighed her name like the sweetest of threats. "You went up in that chopper. You're a photographer. You took pictures and opened a line to MVD headquarters. Of course you have hard copies."

Fear ate at her. If he knew what she had, he'd know precisely how to take it from her as well. She'd seen his work on the vid her drones had captured. He had millennia of experience and no conscience.

He'd kill her in a heartbeat.

Her heartbeat, because he didn't have a heart, didn't have a soul. All this talk of cutting a deal was just that—talk. He didn't have to bargain with her because he already held all the chips. Fear threatened to choke her again.

He inhaled, his nostrils flaring as if he truly were a beast scenting the air. What did he smell? She wondered. What did he know that she didn't?

"You don't like what you do." He was too perceptive. She hated the adrenaline rush. Hated looking over her shoulder to see what was coming. Maybe that was what made her so damn *good* at what she did, because she never let up. Never let her guard down. Not until she was tucked away behind a door and a lock and she could pull the covers up over her head if she wanted to because, even though she was a grown woman, she knew too well, damn it, that there were things that went bump in the night—and all of them, all of them, had come knocking on her door at one time or another. So fear didn't matter. Or, if it did, she'd *pretend* it didn't.

"It doesn't matter what I like," she said. "I have a job to do, Vkhin." She sat down, hard, because her legs were done holding her up and she was done pretending none of this was happening.

For a long moment, he just watched her. "You know who I am. You've been watching me, Ria. You know what I can do."

"Yeah." There was no point in hiding from the truth. She knew *exactly* what he was capable of doing.

He crouched down in front of her, blocking her view. Those massive shoulders of his shut out the sky and the smoke and all the unwelcome signs that her mission was a complete and total clusterfuck of a failure.

"You don't need to be afraid right now."

"You're telling me you're one of the good guys?" He couldn't possibly mean it. He was one of the Fallen.

He shook his head. "Never make that mistake, baby. Anything, anyone you find here in the Preserves is bad to the core. You don't trust me."

He didn't look bad. He looked big and hard and safe. Nothing was getting through him.

He held out a hand to her. "You come with me, and I'll get you out of here. I'll get you back where you belong."

"Just like that?" She stared at him suspiciously.

"Of course not." His hard, sensual smile wasn't nice. "We both know there's a price tag for my services. You're going to have to pay for your exit ticket."

His hand came up when she didn't take it, one finger tracing the curve of her cheek. Her jaw.

She wanted to lean into that finger, that teasing promise of warmth, but he was Fallen and seduction was just another weapon in his arsenal. They both knew that. "I'm not in a paying frame of mind, Vkhin."

The reality of him was overwhelming. Before, she'd always had the safety buffer of her camera lens between them. Now, here he was. Raw and real. Overwhelming.

"That's too bad." His finger paused, rested against her skin. "You should ask me, Ria."

"Ask you what?" Her lips were dry and sensitive, as if fear or the altitude or some alien desire had left them swollen and unfamiliar. He was watching her, though, as if he were daring her to use her tongue to moisten her skin. Around them, night fell like a dark dream. As the shadows grew, it was just her and this fallen angel, making sensual promises she didn't want. Did she?

"Ask me what I want." His booted foot moved deliberately between hers, a heavy weight between her bent knees. "Maybe, you wouldn't mind paying, Ria," he whispered. His thumb stroked a coaxing circle against the skin of her throat.

"I can't." Arousal hummed through her, making her body heated and slow. She wanted to touch him. Wanted to feel his skin against hers and that was so wrong.

"I think you can." His head lowered towards her. God, would he kiss her? Could she let him? "I think you can do whatever you want."

She couldn't believe that sensual, wicked promise. This wasn't about sex, she reminded herself. This was about her life. Her freedom. He'd come after her chopper, which meant the Fallen not only knew what MVD was up to—they had every intention of stopping it. They were on opposite sides.

"I don't do bonds," she whispered.

His head jerked back, but there was no mistaking the harsh look in his eyes. "That's just fine," he growled, "because neither do I. I'm not part of this deal we're making."

Disappointment flooded her, making her wonder what was wrong with her. He was a Fallen angel and he wanted something from her, but what he *didn't* want was a bond.

It wasn't as if rejection was something new.

She shouldn't have felt hurt. Shouldn't have been imagining what it would be like to bond with this male.

"You took photos," he repeated, standing up and moving back as if he couldn't wait to put some space between them. Which was fine. It really was. "And I'm offering you a trade. One exit ticket from this hell your ass is stuck in—in exchange for the pics you snapped.:

"You won't leave me here," she said confidently.

He smiled. A slow, mean smile. "Now, darling, what makes you think that?" She didn't trust him, but clearly he had to get her out because she'd already uploaded the photos. Didn't he?

"You want my photos."

He shot her an inscrutable look. "I could kill you right now, Ria," he pointed out. "If you had time to pop the vidstick on that camera of yours, you'll have secured it somewhere on your person. I could strip you right now, find that card for myself." He shrugged. "Or kill you and dispose of your body. I have lots of options—the one who doesn't have any options in this scenario is you. You have exactly one choice—whether or not you trust me. If you want to get out of here alive, you're going to choose to trust me."

"You'll take me out of here?"

"I'll get you over the wall," he said. "You'll go home."

"Without my pics," she groused.

He reached down and held out a hand again. "Make up your mind," he ordered. "You trust me and you go home. It's that simple, Ria."

Pale white lines from old injuries cut through that sun-darkened skin, scars he'd carry with him forever—and forever was a damned long time when you were near-immortal. Strong, blunt fingers. Capable fingers. Capable of anything, she reminded herself, but there was no escaping the searing heat of the memories of those fingers touching her skin. Holding her in place. He could do whatever she wanted. Anything.

So why was she thinking about taking his offer?

The noise warned her first.

Vkhin dropped his hand, reached for his weapons.

Growls echoed from the trees nearest them as a pack of rogues exploded into the clearing. Oh, God. When the rogues had attacked the chopper, all she'd seen was a pack of winged creatures methodically driving the bird downwards. She'd had an impression of cruel wings and size, but now, face to face with what was coming after her, she realized the sneak peek hadn't prepared her for the reality.

The rogues were big, tough bastards with dark, malformed faces. It was as if someone had brutalized a Neanderthal, making the male harsher, more malevolent. Twisting familiar human features into something purely bestial. The eyes were the worst, though. Those eyes were colder than cold, pure hollow emptiness that advertised the stone-cold killer within.

She didn't want them anywhere near her.

This was why she needed him. Not for sex but for survival. She didn't want to die here and he was the only one who could help her.

"Take cover," Vkhin snapped. She looked wildly around. He had to stop giving impossible orders. Not that she took orders, but there *was* no cover. Just a handful of scrawny trees, a really inhospitable looking cluster of rocks and the deflated chute. Where did he think she was going to go?

There was nowhere safe.

Ruthlessly, he palmed his blades and slammed into the rogue nearest him. Those black eyes of his were pure ice as he methodically cut down the first wave of rogues. Those twin blades of his sliced, ripping through flesh and tore apart bone and sinew until blood painted the ground and trees. The thick copper stink choked her lungs when she sucked air in desperately. The powerful blows were a stark reminder he was a powerful ancient and he wasn't human. She wanted to squeeze her eyes shut, to pretend this was just a bad sim, but she was tired of hiding. Tired of waiting for other people to fight her battles for her. Although Vkhin looked more than capable.

Moving with lethal swiftness, he pulled more blades, the vicious edges driving into the attacking rogues.

The rogues were monsters, clawing and lunging for her strange protector. Why should she trust him? How could she? From where she was, he didn't look all that different from their attackers. A little less dark, but the same ferocious rage twisted his features, drove him forward. He was pure violence incarnate and that made him bad, bad news.

I should run, she thought. He was distracted. She had a chance.

She took two steps away from the trees. Freedom beckoned. She should take it.

No.

She stopped.

No more running.

"Get down," Vkhin roared. When Ria didn't follow orders, he hooked a hand in the collar of her jumpsuit and tossed her behind him. The Preserves' rocky terrain made a decent hidey-hole, with enough good-sized boulders to give some cover. Ria Morgan was a small female and she'd fit if she kept that stubborn head of hers down and out of trouble. Off-balance, she hit the ground harder than he liked, but bruised was preferable to dead.

He'd make it up to her later.

Right now, though, he got himself between her and their incoming, praying to a God who'd given up on him millennia ago that Ria Morgan had the good sense to stay down.

The immediate movement behind him, as she scrambled to her feet, warned him she wasn't the staying put kind. Fuck. He'd deal with her, but first he had business to take care of. A quick scan of the males coming out told him he needed to make every blow count. Four rogues front and center, and they probably had a few more fighters hanging back to take care of clean up. That was just fine with him. He'd been jonesing for a fight since he'd watched Ria's chopper go down.

Adrenaline and fury rushed through him and it felt good to palm the blade. He didn't understand why, but Ria Morgan was *his*. He knew this in his bones, in the dead organ that had been his heart so long ago. She belonged with him and the Dominion he'd been before he'd Fallen wasn't letting anyone take her from him.

"Come and get me," he growled, surveying their attackers. Bastards had blades and guns and their first shot took out his comm. Well, fuck. He hadn't planned on doing an SOS, but he'd wanted to confirm the pick up details before he headed out with Ria. He wasn't going to be doing that now.

That just pissed him off further. Launching a throwing star with lethal accuracy, he took out that anger on the responsible party. Gun went flying as the rogue dropped. Not dead, yet, because the only surefire way to take out one of Heavens' bad boys was to cut off his head, but the bastard wasn't going to be getting up any time soon, either. Worked for him.

"I've got your back," she said and he glared behind him. She'd got that damned pack of hers open, her hands rifling through the contents while her eyes stared at the carnage happening around her. This was not her fight and she could damn well stay where he'd put her.

"You move," he said harshly, "and you won't like the consequences. You understand me, Ria?" If she stayed down, stayed put, those rocks would give her some protection.

She must have read the truth on his face because she nodded, wide-eyed. Yeah. She looked at him and what she saw was one hundred percent killer. He bared his teeth and lunged for the first rogue.

***

The fight was brief but impossibly brutal. Vkhin gutted two of their attackers, then snapped the neck of the third. Inhaling, she got the Glock out and squeezed off a round.

The fourth rogue dropped hard, a red circle blossoming in the center of his forehead. She looked around wildly. She'd *shot* him. And it felt right. She was shaking, but this was something she had to do for herself. She was done sitting around. *Hiding*. He hadn't been human, she reminded herself. And he definitely hadn't harbored friendly intentions.

She fired again when the body twitched, the rogue rolling onto his side and levering himself upright. "Die, you bastard," she hissed.

More red blossoms spread across the rogue's chest. The monster staggered but didn't stay down.

"No," Vkhin snapped. The gun flew out of her hand as he turned in her direction, his arm sweeping into hers. Fingers stinging. "You want to advertise our presence here, you keep right on firing. And bullets won't kill him. You take his head off, he dies. Anything else and he's coming back after you eventually. You put him down, you make sure he stays down."

With brutal economy, he reached down and finished off the rogue she'd shot with a quick drag of knife across the male's jugular. She looked away as the head came off and Vkhin tossed it to one side.

"Now," he growled, "I believe we were discussing your options. Or lack thereof."

Swinging her around, he pinned her against a tree and ruthlessly kissed her.

CHAPTER THREE

Vkhin's kiss was as unexpected as it was hard. Demanding a response she couldn't deny him. She'd been ambushed by a master. His mouth came down on hers, covering her lips as his tongue ruthlessly parted her lips and pushed inside. She'd expected brutality, not the erotic tease. Sure but not rough. Like he knew *exactly* how wet she was.

One big hand slid into her hair angling her head, his thumb ruthlessly nudging her jaw lower so he could take more. That erotic stroke was an unexpected pleasure. *God.* She could get used to this. He tasted like sage and spice, of the outdoors and something entirely, primitively masculine.

He got her pinned between his large body and the tree and she should have been protesting. Should have shoved at him because things like this didn't happen to her and they certainly weren't supposed to. But her adrenaline and fear needed an outlet and, in Vkhin's arms, the lines between that fear and arousal blurred and blended.

And she loved it.

Adrenaline hit her hard, swamping her with the rush of being *alive* when others were dead because she'd been lucky. Because she'd fought to stay that way.

Now she fought for air, his mouth stealing her breath right away. He'd take more than that, take all of her. He was bad news and she shouldn't be standing there. Shouldn't be leaning into him, her fingers curling around his shoulders as she just stood there and *felt*. Felt him, felt the rough-soft brush of his mouth against the sensitive skin of her face. He kissed her and kissed her, his mouth open against hers, his tongue driving into her mouth the way she suspected she wanted his body on hers. In hers.

That unexpected, unspeakable pleasure burned right through her. She didn't want to lose the contact, so she pulled him into her body and he came, giving her the heavy weight of his body against hers. He shifted, advanced, pressing one thickly muscled thigh against the apex of her thighs. And she melted, parting around him.

The sound of his breathing filled her ears. Harsh and rough. Aroused. He wanted her.

Then he drew back, his teeth nipping at her lower lip until the sharp pleasure-pain shot straight to her pussy. Her clit throbbed in time with the small pulse in her lip. When he lifted his head, all she wanted was to pull him back. Arousal made her almost painfully aware of him. If she was dying out here, she'd die with a smile on her face. She reached up, to touch the almost invisible mark on her lower lip, to reach out for him—and he wrapped her wrists in one large hand, pulling out plastic cuffs.

Hell, no.

"Last chance to negotiate. We can do this the hard way, sweetheart." The stroke of that plastic along her skin shouldn't have been so sexy. "Or, you can give me what I want."

Somewhere too close, something large and fuel-heavy exploded, the sound pushing out towards them. Her mind did a three sixty, traveling right back to the chopper and Lieutenant Jones. Had the other woman made it out in time? Or was her body inside the burning wreckage right now? Fuck her wrists and whatever game he thought he was playing with her. She was kissing one of the Fallen while her fellow agents died. Arousal drained away, replaced by grief and anger.

"What happened to the others?" she asked fiercely, pulling at her wrists. "You have to know. Did they get out?"

"What do you think happened?" he rasped. The plastic cuffs snapped effortlessly into place, proving she was no match for his strength. "MVD sends a chopper into Fallen airspace, bad shit happens, sweetheart. Your chopper is down."

"There were two *people* on that chopper." He knew. He had to know.

For a moment, she thought he was going to try to bargain with her. She didn't know what she would have done then, but instead he simply reached over and fastened her wrists to a branch over her head. She didn't resist because she wanted the information he had, pushing her fingers into the bark and hanging on. Maybe, he'd give her what she needed, the information she wanted so desperately. Maybe, he wouldn't.

Somehow, he left her feeling off-balance and uncertain, and it was just the edge of desire she felt when she was around him. She didn't know what he wanted from her, not really. As she stared at him, he edged her flight gloves down, baring her wrists. The unexpected gesture made her feel strangely naked as he eyed the pale, vulnerable skin between her glove and the sleeve of her flight suit.

"Your pilot never had a chance," he said quietly. His fingers stroked over her exposed skin and her skin jumped at his touch. "He died in his seat, still strapped in. It would have been quick."

Grief overwhelmed her for the man she hadn't known. Now, that pilot would never be more than a quick smile when she'd checked in and then he'd lifted off and they'd been on their way. Whoever he was in his off-hours, he wasn't going home.

"Why didn't you stop that crash?" Memories assailed her. "You should have stopped it."

He retreated from her, his fingers slipping away from her wrist as that mask of icy, disciplined determination slammed back into place. God. The man was seething underneath that calm exterior, a cauldron of unexpected emotions. "I will. But first you have to give me those pictures."

"Too late," she whispered reluctantly. She didn't know if she could bargain with him anyhow, but the truth was, he was too late. "I sent the pics digitally before I jumped."

She shouldn't be regretting that decision. It had been her job to get those pictures out, no matter what. Still, part of her regretted she no longer had that bargaining chip. Part of her wanted to keep playing this too-sexy game of what-if and I-could. She'd watched him for two months on MVD's orders, but she hadn't figured him out. Didn't know if she ever could, and *that* fascinated her even more than his body did.

His slow, satisfied smile warned her even before she caught his words. "Check mate, sweetheart."

She closed her eyes, exhaustion and the events of the day catching up with her. "You intercepted the transmission."

"Yeah." He tested the plastic cuffs and stepped away. "Never got there." His slow, hot once-over of her body made her feel more alive than she had in months. "See, I'm still betting you've got the vidstick on you. Somewhere. I can look for it when I get back." Maybe, that kiss of his had been pure practicality, an easy way to shut her up before their pursuers overheard her argument and honed in on their position. Or, maybe her dark angel wanted *her*.

Lust slammed into her. At least, that was what she told herself as she eyed the zipties securing her wrists. This was a game to him. A deadly, serious game—but a game, nonetheless. She was playing him for her soul and her freedom—two things she couldn't do without.

"We're going to work something out," he threatened, even as a second explosion had his head coming up. "Think about it, Ria. Think really carefully. The rogues are coming for you and I'm the best chance you've got to get out of here. MVD can't help you now."

He tucked the chute around her like a blanket and leaned in. "I'm going to cover your tracks and then I'll be back in ten."

In the next instant, he was gone, leaving her alone to contemplate his warning.

She had ten minutes.

Ten minutes to choose whether she lived or died.

Covering her tracks took less than the promised ten. Ria Morgan was inexperienced and he'd been tracking for millennia. She'd kicked over rocks and pushed through the trees before he'd caught up with her. The signs of her passage he could and did erase, but there wasn't much he could do about the bodies. Even if he'd had the means to make the bodies go missing, an a.w.o.l. pack of rogues would have raised alarms anyhow. Those hadn't been acting on their own and whoever was controlling their strings would have eventually demanded a check in. So he'd move out fast, get Ria Morgan back to her own world before shit hit the fan in his.

That kiss kept replaying in his head. Her mouth had opened up beneath his like the sweetest of night flowers, letting him in just that little bit. The sweet, hot taste of her meant now he had an erection that wouldn't quit and he wanted all the way in. Zer's words were practically permission—*bond with her*—and his cock knew it.

She was right where he'd left her, which was just one advantage of a little bondage. That was a fantasy he didn't need right now, though. Imagining Ria Morgan, tied up, waiting for his cock was pure mistake. She was business and he wasn't fucking with her. She deserved better than that.

He had to let her go.

Still, he wasn't quite prepared for the sight of her. Her head rested against the tree trunk, right where he'd left her because she really was out of choices. Deep, steady in-and-out breathing said she'd spent her ten minutes wrestling her emotions back under control. She jumped and tensed when he stepped back into the clearing, but pretended she hadn't noticed his arrival. He didn't like playing on her fear—even if that sharp emotion made his darker side perk up and take notice—but he didn't have too many choices, either. He needed her ready to deal.

"Time's up," he said, as if he'd run down to the corner store for milk and a dozen eggs. She flinched and he knew his voice sounded flat and unemotional—which was enough of a message, wasn't it? She couldn't keep fucking with him and they both knew it. "You need to make your decision, Ria."

"I can't," she said and her voice was a mere whisper of sound. She cleared her throat, as if she wanted her voice to be bigger, to fill up the space between them, but she was tapped out. "I can't do that, Vkhin. You know who I work for. You know the rules. As long as I'm an MVD agent, I'm not a free agent."

"They don't have to know. You tried to transmit and the transmission got cut off. Maybe you lost the camera when you jumped. Maybe that camera hit the ground a little too hard. There are many reasons why you wouldn't have what they need. Pick a story, Ria, and they don't have to know the truth."

"I don't sell out." Who was she trying to convince?

He shook his head and reached for her wrists. "Everyone does. Everyone has a price."

"Everyone human, you mean," she clarified. He should have left her tied up, because nothing got the point across faster than restraints, but he needed to get her moving fast. So he got out his knife, angling the sharp tip beneath the plastic ties.

He disagreed with her argument, though, and he wasn't feeling polite. "Everyone, Ria. Human. Fallen. We all can be bought if the price is right. We just have to find your price. Hold still," he added as the sharp edge brushed against her exposed skin.

"You're for sale?"

He pulled the blade up, a short, controlled tug. The plastic snapped, leaving .his hand cradling her wrists. "Of course. You think I wouldn't do anything for my brothers, Ria? Anything at all to see them get their wings back and get on with their lives?"

She slid her hands out of his and he let her. He could have stopped her. They both knew that. Only thing she didn't know here was why. "Including come after me for my pictures."

"Including that. Think it over, Ria. Take the night," he added. "If you need to. We'll hit the trail now and you think about my offer."

He hadn't asked her to bond with him. Maybe that omission surprised her, but he didn't fucking care. After all, wasn't that the ultimate purpose of the Fallen here in her world? To seduce and to tempt with their promise of a single, diabolical, all-or-nothing favor? She wouldn't bond with him, but she'd wonder about that dark offer.

She'd admit that much to herself, had probably known since she'd found herself tracking his movements across M City. He'd been more than a target. He'd *interested* her.

He'd get her pictures, though. She'd hand them over before she cleared the wall.

He turned away, as if he didn't care whether or not she followed his lead. After all, if she was being honest with herself, he was her only viable option. "We start walking," he said. "We head for the wall now."

"What about you?" This time, she didn't protest his plan. That was a step in the right direction. She came along with him, let him take the lead here, she'd give him what he needed before they hit the walls and he had to admit the truth. That, now he was inside and on the ground, he couldn't simply climb back over the walls. The wards wouldn't let a Fallen touch the wall—because the Preserves were designed to be a one way ticket.

"This is just a walk in the park, right?" she said bitterly. "Nothing to worry about."

"There's plenty to worry about," he said calmly. "Nothing is safe here. So we're going to head west, right up to the edge of the wall."

"You have a built-in GPS?"

He shot her a look. "Don't need one." He flicked a finger towards the dark night sky. This far from M City, light pollution was at a minimum. Tonight, the sky was a carpet of bright stars, patterns of light and cloud spread as far as she could see. "There's your map."

"I'd rather have the GPS." Folding her arms over her chest, she stared back at him.

"You don't need it." He looked up, his eyes scanning the sky. "Big Dipper is there." He gestured with the tip of his blade. All that lethal beauty focused on the poetry of the night sky—it didn't fit with what she'd expected from him. *He* wasn't what she'd expected. "And, right next door, you've got the North Star."

His star was beautiful, a harsh, sharp pinprick of light in the black sky. She still would have traded it for a GPS. The sun would erase his map and then where would she be?

"You line those up, you know where you're going."

"I don't."

"You do. Now. Something happens to me, you just keep heading in that direction. You'll hit the wall."

"And then what? You think you can get me over that wall? Or do we just stand around at the base and wait?" she asked.

"I'm going to get you to the wall," he countered, "but I can't climb it. Can't even touch it. The wards won't let anyone, anything, paranormal touch the walls—you don't fly, you don't cross. My helo is out of fuel, so we're not flying. Once we're close enough, though, my team will be watching. I'll either help you scale the wall, or they'll drop you a line so you can climb out."

"The wall doesn't have a door? A gate?"

"No." He eyed her calmly. "You're in the Preserves, Ria. We built these walls to keep the Fallen *in*. No one leaves once he's inside, so no doors. No exits. Only way out is over. This was *meant* to be a prison."

He'd come here to take advantage of her fear and isolation, but instead he wanted to comfort her. To tell her that everything was going to be okay here because she could do this. She wasn't falling apart. Her hands shook, but she was keeping the fear under wraps now. He shouldn't have found that self-control seductive, but he did and so he let himself have just a little taste. The soul thirst rode him hard as always, demanding he throw it an emotional snack. Ria's emotions were sharp and strong. And wrong. Even as his thirst eased just a fraction, fed by her fear, he knew that.

A woman like her shouldn't be afraid. She didn't know everything he'd done in the millennia since he'd Fallen, but her pale, set face still reproached him. Yeah, he belonged right here in the Preserves with the other monsters.

So the wry smile she shot him shocked him. She wouldn't admit he scared the piss out of her and he respected that.

"So if you can't go over, why can I?"

"Because the wall's only warded against paranormals," he said patiently. "You're human, Ria. You can touch it, climb over."

They headed out and he knew he'd be counting the miles down. "You let me know if you need anything and we'll stop."

She nodded, matching her pace to his. "I'm not stopping for anything," she vowed and he told himself that was exactly what he needed. He didn't want another opportunity to kiss her, to taste all those emotions she kept so carefully concealed inside her. Desire and fear. An arousal that teased his senses, had him longing for something more.

Longing for Ria Morgan, who deserved far better than him.

So he wasn't stopping and he was getting her home.

If he gave into temptation, if he stopped, he might not let her go.

CHAPTER FOUR

The crash site stank of death and super-heated metal. The sharp copper tang hit the back of Hazor's nose, burning down into his lungs until he was more awake than he'd been in months, hyper-aware of his surroundings and the rogues crawling over the wreckage of the downed chopper. The human still strapped in the pilot's seat was very clearly dead and there was little he could do with that kind of leftover. The emotions had gone with the soul. Now, the fire had burned the body almost beyond recognition, melting the MVD-issue jumpsuit onto the blackened remains.

That made Hazor's job here that much easier.

One less human to tell the world that he'd seen Hazor raising an army here in the Preserves—an army with forbidden wings. If word got out, if the Heavens learned too much about Hazor's activities down here, the archangel who had taught Hazor the secret of restoring the Fallen's wings would also Fall and Hazor would lose his own newly regained wings.

And that wasn't happening.

"There were three humans," Hazor growled.

His second-in-command inhaled sharply and hissed. "Not all dead."

"One dead. Two jumpers. Both female." Hazor pointed to the corpse. "Pilot went down with the bird, but the photographer and the bodyguard jumped clear. First went out about five minutes before the chopper went down. We'll start the search two clicks west of here. The other jumped last minute, so she should be close."

The second jumper wasn't mission critical. She was muscle for the photographer and Hazor doubted the woman had seen anything beyond her targets. If she'd had the vidstick from the camera, she'd have bailed sooner instead of trying to draw the rogues' fire away from her companion. Whatever intel she had was in her head. Taking care of her would be simple.

The photographer was a different story, he realized as he examined the burnt wreckage of the tripod-mounted camera. Fire had gone to work but not before someone had popped the vidstick, which meant whatever info had been on the camera was now walking around the Preserves.

His second snapped his fingers, summoning a tracker to his side. Rezon was a big, hard bastard with a scar that twisted down the left side of his face. Topping out at well over six feet, he towered over the other rogues who cleared a path for him. He was all cold menace and didn't so much as blink when Hazor gave him his orders.

"You take the second jumper." He'd go after the photographer himself.

""Kill or retrieve?" Rezon asked in a flat voice.

"Retrieve." There were advantages to getting his hands on the missing female and you didn't send a tracker like Rezon after a female without clarifying the life-or-death situation. "If you can. If she gives you trouble, kill her. The first girl, however—I want her alive. She'll have the vidstick somewhere on her person." And, even if she didn't, he still needed to make sure. He couldn't allow the information she was carrying to fall into the hands of the Fallen—and he'd fought alongside those bastards for too many years to write them off now. The Fallen would send someone after the chopper.

"Speed," he said, "is of the essence. I want these girls. Now."

Nodding, the tracker peeled off, heading north to find the second jumper. Rezon had never lost a trail yet.

Dismissing the tracker and his quarry, Hazor turned his attention back to the crash site and its surroundings, running his eyes over the deets. Twenty minutes and five hundred yards later and he had his direction. The broken canopy and a minute trace of blood on the trees below said that this was where the photographer had hit the ground. He snapped out an order and a second team took off, running hard on her scent. He'd catch up with them after he'd finished his sweep of the crash site. Just in case there was anything—any *clue*—he was missing here.

Hazor had his orders and they were simple. Kill the girl. She'd seen too much, taken photos of Hazor intoning the runes that gave a rogue back his wings in exchange for a demonic bargain. Maybe, she wouldn't—couldn't—connect those dots. Or, on the other hand, maybe she could. Just maybe, she could repeat the runes and that made her a walking recipe for how to add wings to a Fallen. If that was the case, she couldn't be allowed to leave the Preserves. That information could *not* be allowed to fall into the hands of Zer and his lieutenants.

So the order had gone out.

The human photographer and her companions had to die. Fast or slow, it didn't matter. What did matter was ensuring she never spoke of what she'd seen.

Picking up the trail, he got his ass in gear and moved out, his pack following close on his heels. He'd lead. They'd follow. It was almost too simple, like using an Uzi to shoot fish in a barrel. Too damned easy.

Sucking air deep into his lungs, he memorized the scent and the taste of his prey. Her aura tasted like lemons and orange, ginger and cinnamon. He could almost taste the shock of her crash landing in the middle of a prison. He inhaled again, holding the breath as long as he could. And desire.

The human woman smelled most deliciously of arousal.

The Preserves had been carved out of the broad sweep of Russian steppe. Hundreds of years ago, Cossack fighters had ridden hard across this ground, driving their horses into bloody battles. Now, after the devastation of the Great Wars, the Fallen had bought up the land. There was nothing pretty left here, just a harsh, stony landscape that would have given even the fiercest Cossack warrior pause, all narrow, twisting chutes of rock shot through a barren landscape. Even in the almost impenetrable darkness that had surrounded them when the sun finally gave in and fell beneath the horizon hours ago, Vkhin's long-legged stride ate up the ground like he just couldn't wait to get where he was going. Which was far, far away from her.

Since he'd taken the lead when they'd set off, Ria had plenty of time to think—and to admire the view in front of her. Vkhin's big body was like something straight out of a dream, strong and sure. And that ass of his was something else. She wanted to beg him to take off the leather duster he wore like a suit of armor.

Which she wasn't going to do.

She didn't want to trust him. He had an ulterior motive, as he'd made perfectly clear. He wanted her pics—not her. And yet she was still tempted by him. She could admit that, to herself. She didn't have to say the words out loud, didn't have to give him that truth. He was big. He was brutal. And he was beautiful. She couldn't stop sneaking glances at him, because the reality of Vkhin was so much more than her surveillance footage had shown.

This trip had to be all business. Something was very wrong because her chopper should not have been taken down by winged angels. MVD needed that intel stat, which meant she needed to haul ass, get out and get home. With her vidstick.

Unfortunately, the only life line she had was a Fallen angel with the hardest body she'd ever seen and a chip on his shoulder even she couldn't miss. He'd made it perfectly clear that he didn't like humans. That *she* was trespassing on his territory. And he came with a price tag—she wanted out of here, he was claiming her vidstick for his own.

"Why do you really want my pictures?" She staked her own claim, forcing her hand not to check for the vidstick stashed in her bra. "I understand the Fallen don't want MVD sticking its nose in the Preserves. It's your territory. These are your people. You've all made that perfectly clear. But why would my pics matter? This isn't one of those just-on-principle busts, Vkhin. We both know that."

He didn't slow down, those shitkicking combat boots of his eating up the ground effortlessly. "This isn't about MVD," he said, climbing over a pile of rocks blocking their path.

"Alright." She took the hand he held out to her. His fingers wrapped around her wrist, tugging her up. "They're just pictures," she argued. His fingers were warmth against her own, cooler skin. "Nothing you'd want."

"You have no idea what I want." As soon as her feet were firmly planted, he let go of her wrist.

The section of the Preserves they were field-tripping through must have been inhabited years ago, before the nuclear accidents of the Great Wars had rendered large strips of the Russian countryside uninhabitable by humans. The ground was level here, a rusted-out car abandoned on the edge of their makeshift path. Maybe, there'd been a road connecting A to Z here long ago, before the Fallen had bought up the land and turned it into a paranormal prison. Now, the car's exterior was little more than rust-colored strips of peeling metal. The glass of the windshield had spider-webbed, thousands of cracks rippling outward from the hole in the middle. Somehow, that glass held despite the damage.

"I was shooting out of a moving chopper." She shrugged. "I doubt those shots are too clear. Your boys intercepted them, so you know exactly what I have." Which was more than she did. She'd shot on instinct, her finger on auto-pilot, because she'd needed the barrier between herself and the horror of what was unfolding on the ground.

"It doesn't matter now," he said. "If you don't go over the wall before the rogues catch up, it doesn't matter what you did or didn't see."

"Let's talk about that, shall we?" The kernel of anger was unexpected. She might not be as big or as strong, but she was part of this strange partnership. For some reason, he wanted something *she* had. He wanted—needed—to get her out of the Preserves. She didn't want to think about what would have happened if she hadn't had the photos as a bargaining chip. Nausea curled through her stomach. The winged angels had battered at the chopper like the bird was a toy. She could be dead.

All in all, MVD's recon mission had been a failure. Sure, she'd shot pictures, but what had she really captured? She thought back over the scene on the ground, talking it through out loud. "Tell me when I get close," she suggested. "We fly in—"

"Illegally," he interrupted. "No humans in Fallen airspace. That was the deal, Ria. Whether you knew it or not, your superiors knew it real well. They knew they were sending you on a suicide mission."

Those words of his hurt, probably, she decided, because they were true. She was disposable. Just like always. It didn't matter that *she'd* been sent. Someone had to go—and she'd been handy, like running through a drive-through when the hunger pangs hit and there wasn't enough time to do a sit-down.

"Fine," she said, because there was no point in harping on her role here. "MVD decides they need a closer look at what's going on on the ground in the Preserves because, you see, Vkhin, we've been hearing things. Rumors. Wild stories about flying angels, even though we all know your kind can't fly." What the hell, she decided. Maybe, she'd give him the truth after all. "I spot an anomaly while operating one of the drones—what looks like wingless rogues *flying*— and MVD chain of command decides it merits a second glance. So I go up, in a chopper, and we head for the problem spot. Only, the problem turns out to be that that spot isn't some blank spot on the radar with weird weather. No, what I'm seeing are flying objects. *Angels*, Vkhin, who've got their wings back."

He stopped then and just stared right at her. That hard, black gaze was the most lifeless, soul-less thing she'd ever seen. His eyes were cold as a bitch and she'd clearly connected one too many dots. He didn't like her conclusions. At all. So her breath shouldn't be catching, her eyes shouldn't be moving over the hard planes of his face, wondering how he'd got the small, silver scar on his left cheekbone. He didn't want her, she reminded herself fiercely. She was just the means to an end.

She hated the lack of light, the way the sky overhead was all impenetrable blackness. She stumbled because her night vision wasn't great and cracking open a torch would have been a nice move, but something about the darkness stopped her. That lack of light was menacing. As if something—someone—was watching. She could feel her pulse speeding up, slamming against the skin of her wrist, her throat. In another minute, she'd be fighting to breathe as the world and her chest closed in. *No.*

Don't think about it.

Desperate for something new to think about, a distraction from the darkness, she replayed the scene in her head. So she had proof that some of the rogues had wings. Those wings were no happily-ever-after, but they didn't have to mean Armageddon, either. Half the world would dismiss the pictures as more evidence of media tampering. The other half would rant and rave, but just because a few of the rogues could fly, didn't mean the world was coming to an end.

Did it?

The flying angels had been different from Vkhin in more ways than just the wings. She tried to remember the how and the why of what happened, because she sensed the connection was important.

"The rogue Fallen on the ground—" she said, thinking it out—"not all of them had wings yet." Memory brought back the frantic click of the camera's shutter. She'd zoomed in on one dark shadow. No wings, not at first, just the red runes writhing on the male's scarred back. Forming one by one. "I have the recipe, don't I?" she said flatly. "Those words the winged angel was chanting—those are the magical step by step instructions on how to put a pair of wings back on a Fallen angel. I look at those pictures and figure out how to pronounce the runes, I can add wings to any of the Fallen."

"Maybe," he allowed. "But you're not sharing those pictures with anyone, Ria. You have to keep what you know to yourself."

That wasn't going to be a problem.

"So why not just kill me?" She had to say it, because that was the elephant in the room, wasn't it? She was alone with him. He'd already made it perfectly clear that he was bigger, stronger. Meaner. Snapping her neck would mean a handful of seconds to him—and whatever knowledge she had would be far more than off-limits to MVD.

"I don't want you dead, Ria." There was no mistaking the hungry look in his eyes, however. He wanted something.

At least the unfriendlies following their asses hadn't caught up and the lack of light would put them out of business until daylight, too. The last winged rogue had disappeared from the horizon a half hour ago. Maybe, they had an all clear for the moment. Vkhin risked a glance back at his companion and knew he had to call it. She was game, but no way she went any further. Not without a couple of hours to catch her breath. Plus, that new limp of hers screamed blister, too.

He could afford to give her an hour or two to rest, then they needed to be on the move again.

Didn't take long, either, to find a decent place to stop and hunker down once he'd started looking.

"We're stopping?" Her voice slurred with exhaustion as she trudged towards him. "I thought you wanted me to put out."

He ignored her last suggestion, but couldn't shake the fantasies running through his head. He was supposed to be cold. Unfeeling. He'd spent millennia serving as Zer's right hand. He was a warrior. He fought and he killed—and he had no fucking regrets about that. So he shouldn't feel this hunger for Ria Morgan. From the first moment he'd felt her watching him, he'd felt *something* however, a complicated mix of hunger and lust and an unfamiliar, unwanted tenderness.

He needed those pics. That was all this was.

He was only stopping because she was human and therefore fragile. Of course, if she bonded with him, that wouldn't be an issue anymore. But he didn't want to bond with anyone.

"I might have another mile in me," she said. He watched her put one foot in front of the other like she'd been drunk for a week and hadn't figured out the straight line deal. Yeah. Definitely time to call it quits. Whatever she had left wasn't much at all.

"Park it," he said and she stumbled to a halt, almost body-slamming him in her haze of exhaustion.

"You're quitting now?" She set her pack down, though, and followed it to the ground.

"You ask too many questions," he grumbled. His knife sliced clean through the branch, peeling the fibers off in long strands. He'd peeled rogues like that, let their screams wash right on over him because he had a job to do and intel to gather. She didn't know what kind of a monster she was prodding.

Before he could say something he'd regret, he got busy with his blade again and cuts a dozen long poles, lashing them together into a primitive frame. The raw cuts would advertise their presence, but speed was going to win the day tomorrow, not stealth.

She flipped open the bag, rummaging around inside it. "And you don't answer any of them."

"You're tired." He covered the frame he'd made with the tough nylon chute she'd jumped with. Kind of teepee-like, he decided. Wasn't the Ritz-Carlton, but, with the opening tucked at a right angle to the rising wind, she'd be out of the cold and damp. That was worth half a star right there. Her eyes followed him as he did his thing, undoubtedly full of more questions.

"How come you don't want to do that bonding thing?"

"You volunteering?"

Her mouth snapped shut. "Not really."

She hadn't, he noticed, denied the possibility flat out. Instead, she dropped her gaze and began rummaging around inside that bag of hers again. Eventually, she pulled out a granola bar and tore open the silver wrapper. He wished he could give her the doughnut and coffee he knew she craved, but there were some things he couldn't do.

"You want one?" she asked.

"I'm good for now." He collected a handful of rocks to weigh down the edges of the chute. Too bad he wasn't a Boy Scout, because this was merit badge material right here. "You got more water in that bag of yours, you should drink it. Make sure you don't dehydrate."

She chewed and swallowed. "This all part of the protect-and-evac deal you offered? A little hospitality for the night and you make sure I eat and drink?"

He stepped away from the skeleton he'd assembled. The branches would hold the chute nicely. Might not be the prettiest place she'd ever slept, but she'd be okay for tonight.

"You don't want to bond with me," he pointed out. "What you want is to get out of here. Preferably in one piece."

"In one piece is good." She nodded and took another bite of granola bar. "That's a plan I could get behind."

"So give me what I want and it's all yours."

"Right." She fell silent, methodically chewing through the remainder of her bar.

The bond mate biz was hardly a secret. Humans traded their souls for a favor. Money, a promotion, power over someone else. They loved that shit, loved what they could get. And the Fallen had to meet the price tag.

Because when you had a bond mate, you could experience that mate's emotions second-hand. Like a drug. Temporarily fill up the void inside the Fallen angel. When Michael had ripped away their wings, he'd also ripped out their ability to feel the finer things in life, and Vkhin wasn't talking opera and vintage Champagne. All the nicer emotions except for the brutish, feral, *killing* ones. His last mate's face flashed through his head, right on queue, as if he needed the reminder. There were some things, some people, a male didn't forget. Ever.

The Fallen came all pre-addicted. If they didn't get their fix, their killer instincts came out. Army of rogues tearing up M City was proof enough of that.

A soul mate was something—*someone*—else entirely. There was one pre-destined woman for each Fallen angel. Find her, take her, love her—and the warrior re-grew his wings and his all-access pass to the Heavens. He got a cosmic do-over and a second chance. He and his new mate were also bound together for all eternity. Problem was, the archangel Cuthah had had his own plans for taking over the Heavens and he hadn't wanted the Fallen to get that second chance, so he'd methodically killed off every single soul mate he could find. In three thousand years, the Fallen had found precisely three. *Three.* So Vkhin wasn't standing in line waiting for this woman to show up.

He didn't need to.

The temptation to let go was too damned strong.

He was used to carving out a life. Life in the Preserves wasn't that fundamentally different from his life back in M City—it was all about living life on the edge. All about survival. She didn't belong here. Which was just as true as the fact that he did belong here, even if something inside him was coming alive. Something he'd thought dead and buried.

"Well, fuck," she said and that about summed it up. He leaned forward and got a good look at her face. The cold and dark had done a number on her and there was no missing the dazed look in her eyes. Damned, too, if her lips weren't tinged with blue. This conversation was over.

"We'll sleep inside." When he flipped open the flap for her, she hesitated.

"Give me a minute," she said, her cheeks pinkening with something other than cold.

Fair enough. He wouldn't make her say it. Going inside, he left the flap up while he got a small fire going inside. He could hear her rustling around outside, taking advantage of the bushes. Five minutes before he'd planned to go after her, she stuck her head inside. Watching.

She didn't back away, so he kept on working, pushing the hot coals deep into the ground. Those coals would keep her warm while she slept. He dropped a Mylar blanket from the survival kit over the lot, reaching for her.

She came, letting him draw her down onto the silver blanket.

"We'll rest here for a couple of hours. Then, we move out." He handed her a bottle of water. "Drink."

She made a face but complied. Again. He wondered how far he could push that luck. "Will they find us?"

He shook his head. "Not tonight. We're under cover here and we've got a head start." Tomorrow, yeah. Tomorrow, they'd be in deep shit unless they hit that wall fast. Tonight, however, she was safe enough. "I'm going to go back out there," he told her. "Nothing gets in here."

She yawned. "Except through you."

"Precisely."

He tucked his leather duster around her, crouching over her in a long-sleeved black shirt and pants. "You're good at this, aren't you?" Her face looked up at him through the shadows. Exhausted, he reminded himself. *Vulnerable*, his inner beast calculated.

"I should be." He slipped her hair back behind her ear. "I've been doing this for three thousand years."

"Stay with me." She yawned again as he pulled her against his larger, harder body. He shouldn't. Christ, he knew that. He should leave.

Instead, he followed her down onto that damned blanket.

CHAPTER FIVE

"Just a little. A little taste." His voice was a harsh growl in her ear. She should have backed the hell away from him, but instead she was wet just listening to him. He didn't want to do this. He'd made that perfectly clear, but tempting that control of his was tempting her and, just this once, she was going to take what she wanted. And she'd wanted Vkhin since he'd emerged from the shadows. Before that, too, if she was being honest. She'd been fighting the sensual hunger he aroused in her and now? She was just hungry. For him.

"You're a tease." Just to make her point, she arched backwards against him, curling into his heat. He was driving her crazy and he hadn't even touched her yet. Not really. But her pussy was wet and swollen and she wanted him to touch her there. Wanted to feel his fingers in her and on her.

"Tell me what you want, Ria." He lowered his head, pressing his mouth against the soft, vulnerable skin where her neck met her shoulder. She could feel his muscles, the strength of him as he shifted behind her, adjusting their fit until they were skin to skin. "Maybe," he whispered against her skin, "you'd enjoy just my fingertips—just a little."

She whimpered, softening against him. Heat blazed through her, scorching her face, her breasts. And lower. She knew her panties were soaked. What would it be like when he finally gave in and touched her, reached beneath the damp cotton and sank into her heat? She wanted him too badly to wait any longer.

"You have to ask for it," he warned. "That's the deal."

He was killing her with the desire blazing between them. Waiting wasn't what she wanted. "That's your deal." Her voice was hoarse, unrecognizable to her own ears. She was changing, here in the dark and in his arms, becoming some other woman. She should have been frightened by the effect he had on her but the sensations filling her were too sweet, too hot. All she wanted was *more*.

She parted her legs, sensation uncurling in her. "Are you sure?"

"Yeah." His voice was hard and uncompromising behind her. He thought he'd scared her off.

Fine. Two could play at this game. "I could ask you—" She licked her lips. It was dark inside the retreat he'd built for her, but instinct warned her he could see her just fine. Was watching her. A naughty thrill zinged through her. She could give him something to watch.

She didn't want to be alone, fighting to make it out of the Preserves with murderous rogues tracking her. Those rogues caught up and her forbidden attraction to Vkhin was going to be the least of her problems. She couldn't count on anything but this handful of moments, wrapped in the dark and the warmth of this male's arms. Maybe he wasn't offering a happily ever after or even more than just this one night, but she didn't want to be left alone here and he was the only exit she had.

He shifted behind her. The smell of leather filled their shelter as he tucked that duster of his closer around her. "Ask me, Ria." That sexy growl convinced her. "Whatever you want, all you have to do is ask."

Dropping her head back onto his shoulder, she tried to look up at him but she was no cat and their shelter was dark. All she could make out was the shadowy outline of his face. She'd seen him on vid like this a dozen times or more. Hard. Knowing. He'd fought for the Fallen, fought to keep M City safe from the rogues. He might be Heavens' bad boy, but he'd done everything in his power to stay on the right side of the line in the fight against M City's monsters. He wasn't good, but he wasn't the bad guy, either. The lines that had been drawn in this battle weren't that simple. Now, wrapped in his arms, the lines were blurring even further.

His mouth moved against her neck, a hot, seductive glide of male skin and warmth that promised more. Much more.

"I shouldn't." *God, she shouldn't.* She was hyper-aware of his arms, hands. He hadn't moved an inch, still and waiting. He was all predator, stalking her like the sweetest of prey. The thick ridge of his erection pressed against her backside, making her deliciously aware of his strength through the layers of clothing separating them.

"Probably not," he agreed as his mouth found her ear. He was her anchor in the darkness. Comfortable and yet strangely familiar. She'd watched him for weeks, but he kept to himself too much. Even when he'd hunted with his fellow Fallen, he was reserved, those dark eyes shuttered and wary. She hadn't learned anywhere near enough to satisfy the curiosity burning through her.

"I've been watching you," she admitted. He'd gone about his business in M City in that long duster and the worn blue jeans that clung to his muscled thighs with each sure, confident move that he'd made. He'd prowled the alleys, meting out the Fallen's own brutal brand of justice, and she'd watched. Every night, she'd watched him go out and fight, and she'd fought the urge to follow him back to his base when he'd finished. To strip off those jeans and see what he was hiding beneath the worn fabric.

"I know," he rumbled. "Tell me what you saw, Ria."

"I've seen you fight." His tongue explored the curve of her ear. Tasting her like he could eat her up. She shivered, because, oh, God, his touch was pure wickedness. She shouldn't have felt that simple touch so strongly, but she did.

She'd never seen him take a woman. Countless times, she'd seen his brothers, the other Fallen, do that, seen them wrap themselves around a woman and take her. Hard and fast and thorough, until that woman had thrown back her head and screamed from the pure pleasure of it all. Something happened during those pairings and she'd recognized their lovers' satisfied smiles. Secretly wanted that for herself with Vkhin. "But I've never seen you with a lover."

"Not while you've been watching. Not for a long time, Ria."

"Why not?" She shouldn't be asking this, she knew.

"I'm dangerous," he growled. "Don't ever forget that."

"Maybe I like dangerous."

"You like it safe, Ria." His fingers touched her cheek. "You like to watch, baby, from your nice, safe desk while you control everything around you. That's not dangerous at all."

Maybe she was tired of always playing it safe. Her fingers clenched on the front of her jumpsuit, crumpling the fabric. Nothing about Vkhin was safe. He woke a side of her she hadn't known existed. He made her feel alive. Curious.

Heated.

Safe or not, she wanted the male holding her in his arms. So she slid her own hand down over her stomach. "I have to ask you, Vkhin?"

"Yeah," he growled.

"But I can take care of myself." That was a delicious thought. She could. She could do this, with or without him.

He cursed, low and hard behind her and, God, that erection of his just got impossibly larger. She was teasing the beast. She knew he wouldn't hurt her. She had his promise. She'd have to ask him for what she wanted. He wasn't taking.

So, why not do this? Why not play this game with him and try living—just a little—dangerously? Her hand found her pussy through the heavy fabric of her jumpsuit. Swollen. Needy. The first simple, soft stroke sent a sharp burst of pleasure through her clit. It felt good, so she did it again, pushing against her own finger. The male behind her froze right up.

"Ria —" he groaned and her name sounded like a prayer on his lips.

"Shhh," she whispered. "Little busy here." She drew her finger through the heavy folds, pressing the fabric inwards with just enough pressure to have her hips rocking forward, savoring the teasing pressure of her own finger. A delicious, slow heat unfurled

inside her.
She stroked.
Hard masculine hands covered hers. "Ask me," he demanded.

Vkhin's body went nuclear. The woman in his arms wasn't lost, wasn't unsure. No, she was taking what she wanted from him and that was the sexiest thing he'd ever seen. Her face tipped back against his shoulder because she was doing some watching of her own right now. Whatever she read on his face, she liked, because she gave that slow smile of hers, stretching against him and sliding her hands free of his.

His cock got harder, the tip damp. God, she was good.

Good in more ways than one. He wasn't supposed to want her. And, even if he did, he reminded himself, this was just lust. He didn't need anything else from her besides those damned pictures so he shouldn't be holding his breath when she reached for the zipper on her flightsuit. Her fingers wrapped around the little metal tab and teased it down an inch. The back of her fingers brushed the creamy skin she revealed and he wanted to replace that hand with his mouth.

"I'll show you," she said throatily, nudging that damned zipper down another inch. She unzipped the flight suit as if she were unwrapping a Christmas present, one teasing inch at a time. The sight of that lacy bra she'd been hiding beneath the utilitarian nylon and cotton made him want to tear the wrappings right off of her. Lilac satin cupped her breasts, her hard little nipples peeking over the lace-trimmed edges. Those nipples of hers were the color of summer raspberries and hard with her need.

"These," she whispered, brushing her fingers against her nipples. "Maybe, I want you to touch me right here." Hell, yes, he wanted to touch her. He wanted to taste her nipples, tongue her until he'd learned whether she tasted like raspberries or not and she understood exactly what she wanted from him. He didn't deal in uncertainties. Ever.

His hands gripped her hips, spanning the delicate bones with his hands. She was human, fragile and he couldn't let himself forget that. He needed to remember the consequences of kissing her. Because she tempted him more than any woman he'd ever held and his control was already too tenuous.

"Maybe?" he growled. "Let me know when you've made up your mind, Ria."

Her fingers brushed over her own nipples and the little hum of feminine satisfaction undid him. He could give her more, but he shouldn't. His fingers flexed, his thumb stroking little circles against the soft curves of her stomach as the emotions poured from her. Her aura was as wild and hesitant, as fiery, as a good sunset. He'd watched more than his fair share of sunsets, felt the blaze of heat and color slipping away to be replaced with night. He'd been alone in the dark for thousands of years. He knew better than to reach for that heat of hers, but he couldn't lose her. Not yet.

He brushed his mouth against her skin again, tasting the pulse that beat strong and bright against his lips. That fire of hers undid him.

"Are you ready for me, Ria?"

Her head pushed back against his shoulder, her hands finding his wrists and holding on. He was already lost, his hands moving, pulling apart the jumpsuit, baring all her pretty skin for his touch. He fought for control, a grimace pulling the corners of his lips back. He wanted this to be good for her. To give her what she needs. He could sense all too clearly the need in her. The loneliness. Christ, he understood those emotions too well. When her hands had gone to his wrists, he'd been prepared for her to push him away. He'd go, too. He'd played many sensual games, but he'd never forced a woman and he wasn't starting tonight.

Instead, she held on. She didn't let go of him at all, the sweet heat of her passion rolling over him as she shocked him by guiding his hand closer. Deeper. Harder. That seductive confidence was his undoing.

"I think you are," he growled, sliding his hand down the rounded curve of her belly and over the little lilac panties. She was soaking wet. Blazing hot. Boldly, he caressed that lace-covered mound, drawing his finger down the tempting crease.

"Yes," she said, pressing her mound against his hand. Her thighs parted, opening up for him and he repeated the caress, dragging his finger through those lace-covered folds, rubbing the fabric against her slick flesh. Her juices saturated the cotton, her bare skin temptingly close.

She was supposed to be an MVD agent, all buttoned up and play-by-the-rules. He was in charge here. But he wasn't. Somehow, she'd got him wrapped around her fingers. She'd watched him for months, but he'd been watching her, too. Learning her. And Ria Morgan liked to watch. Liked to tease.

And, apparently, she liked to sin.

He pressed his erection against her sweet ass and she opened up more, letting his hand slip deep and cup her. The spicy sweet scent of her exploded through his senses as his fingers found her fiery heat. She was wet where she pressed against him, rubbing those soft folds against his fingers. Demanding more.

He could give her that. "I'll make this good," he promised, taking the zipper down further with his free hand. He wanted to see this, to see her opening up for him, letting him in. He pulled her closer, taking in the sight of his fingers on her lacy panties, a dark shadow against the delicate lavender. The shadow of dampness teased him where the panties dipped low beneath the soft curve of her belly, skimming her mound to curve up her ass. Those panties of hers were wicked and provocative and all he wanted was to tear them off her.

"You can," she said, as if she could read his mind, as if they had truly bonded and her feelings were open to him. "If you want to."

He did. He wanted to flip her over, take her deep and hard. Feel every inch of her silky channel clinging to him. That particular fantasy wasn't happening. Not tonight. His erection strained against his pants, begging to get closer, but he wasn't an animal. And she wasn't ready for him.

She moved demandingly against his hand, sensations shuddering through her. "Can you feel it, too?"

"Yeah," he said roughly. "Just like that, baby." His fingers stroked rhythmically down her center, pressing the damp fabric inwards with small, teasing strokes that fed her building hunger. Urged her higher.

"Vkhin." Her eyes closed, her breath catching. She was close, so close, and he wanted nothing more than to watch her go over that edge and find the pleasure waiting for her. He could feel the little tremors starting in her legs, her pussy, as the hunger built and she got close, so close. That little noise she made in her throat had him working a deeper, harder pattern on the damp lace.

Her hips arched and he drank in the hum of feminine approval. Her quiet, lush enjoyment of his attention.

"Let go for me, baby," he whispered roughly. "Enjoy this for me."

Reaching around her, he hooked her leg around his. The heat of her leg seared him where she pressed against him, the feel of her burning through the fabric of his combat pants. Those lavender panties framed by the opened jumpsuit were the most beautiful sight he'd ever seen. He wanted to strip the lace off, bare her for his touch. His kiss. Not yet, he thought desperately, reaching for control.

Fabric rustled as she arched upwards. The muscles in her thighs bunched, clenching as she lifted up into his touch. *Now.* Her clit was a hard little pearl when he thumbed her, stroking over the sensitive skin. She gasped, her nails digging into his arm, and he touched her again and again, driving her towards. He had to look, had to look down at her fire-dappled body. Shadows danced across that creamy, bare skin.

He couldn't take her, he reminded himself desperately. Not here. On the ground. When she was fighting the unfamiliar rush of adrenaline and fear.

She came fast, pushing into his hand as she came apart. Savage satisfaction filled him and he drove his thumb over her hard, needy little clit, his fingers playing with her opening through the thin fabric of her panties. As she closed her thighs around his hand, holding him to her, he eased the tip of one finger beneath the elastic.

"Yes," she groaned. She was hot and slick where he touched her, the spicy-sweet scent of her overwhelming him.

He kept just his finger there. Not demanding. Testing. Waiting for her to decide to accept him. When she did, lifting up to ride the tip of him, he petted at her gently, letting his thumb slide inside her just a fraction. She was tight and wet, her body rising and falling against his as her flesh clenched around him. She gave a choked cry, as if the first little throb had surprised her, but then she was bucking against his fingers, driving herself down, inch by heated inch onto his waiting finger. Like he wanted her to take his cock.

She came in long, hard spasms, her emotions overwhelming him with each strong, short beat. Desire and pleasure. She let go, came apart in his arms and her mind opened up with her body, sucking him in. He was inside her head before he could stop himself. Heat and need. A slow, heated return to awareness as the pleasure eased up. Confusion. *Fear.*

Don't be afraid, he whispered inside her mind before he could stop himself. *Let me*, he coaxed. Christ, she was delicious. So alive. He drank in the smallest taste of those emotions of hers, all that he could without a bond between them. He was an addict falling off the sober train and deliriously, temporarily, happy about that fall.

She shoved away from him, rolling. The duster trapped her arms, pinning her down.

The hunger beat at him, demanding he feed it. Feed on her. Drink those emotions he could sense, taste, so clearly from her and replace the shame and the need with something else.

Something of her.

"Get. Out." She scrambled away from him, fighting the confines of his coat and his arms. Desperately, he fought to process her words, to push back the red haze, the voracious thirst riding him. She wanted him out of her head. Stat. He pulled back, crouching on the edges of all those emotions.

"Bastard." Her eyes glinted up at him, shiny with tears. The second time he'd made her cry today. He ran a finger down her pale cheek, tracing the angry track. He'd known better. He was an animal who couldn't be trusted, because he'd done this before. Lost control before.

Shoving the memories back, Vkhin let Ria roll away from him, let her put a handful of inches between them. There was nowhere she could go to escape him, not here. Not with the night outside their shelter and a pack of rogues on their asses. He knew it and she knew it, but he let her move away to preserve the illusion that she still had a choice and he still had control of the thirst.

He hadn't feared anything in millennia—death and pain and a complete lack of the finer emotions made damned sure of that. But Ria Morgan scared the hell out of him. She'd thought about the bond. He could see it in her eyes, hear the unspoken question in every word she spoke. She might not want that connection—yet—but she'd done some thinking. Worse, if she asked long enough, he'd give in and give it all up to her. He wanted *this*, the tenuous emotional connection he could feel forming between them. That fragile emotional bond was more sensual, more tempting than any skin-to-skin he'd ever had. There was just something about *her* and he was a selfish bastard who wanted just that last, little taste.

Of her.

Then, he'd go. Let it all go.

It wouldn't be hard at all out here to die.

CHAPTER SIX

The smell of fresh blood was a wake-up call even before Hazor spotted the bodies. It was pitch black now and he needed to stop for the night, because he ran the risk of missing their tracks now that he'd lost the light.

The stink of fresh blood, however, was too obvious to ignore. That was the stink of fuck-up and failure, which meant he was going to be stopping for a little Q&A.

And, of course, the bodies belonged to the first team of rogues he'd sent after Ria Morgan. If he'd gone with them in the first place, would the outcome have been different? Or would he be dead, too, his blood polka-dotting the clearing when his head parted company with his body? He wanted to believe he'd still be doing the inhale-exhale, but he hadn't achieved his current rank by closing his eyes to the truth, either.

While he'd stayed behind to secure the crash site and wipe it clean—because the Fallen weren't getting that free investigative pass when they sent in their own team—someone had got the jump on him. Fuck. Calling his rogues a team was stretching it—his fighters would happily disembowel each other to keep the wings Hazor had bestowed on them—but the numbers still should have meant something. The four dead rogues had certainly had the very human, very female Ria Morgan outgunned and outpowered. No way a little desk jockey took out four fallen angels by herself.

Which meant there was a whole lot of other shit going on here. Gritting his teeth, he sucked in the scent and considered his next move. He'd fed earlier, and the raw, pounding thirst was gone. Only temporarily, of course. Thirst would be back, but he had enough time to finish this job before he needed to hunt for something more personal. Plenty of time to admit to himself that what he hadn't anticipated were the Fallen *beating* him to the scene. His nemesis wasn't behind him. No, he was goddamned out in front and leading by a mile.

Because a Fallen warrior had already picked up Ria Morgan.

He crouched down, examining the ground. Damp made it easier to read the traces of footmarks marking up the fight's site, but someone real professional had taken the time to erase her backtrail. Those footprints cut off as soon as he moved away from the scene which left him with a whole lot of nothing to go on. Ria Morgan was just gone, right off the grid, and all he had were the bodies.

The logical course was to take Ria Morgan straight to the wall, because if the Fallen had had any other means of air-lifting her ass out of here, Hazor would have seen the air traffic. So all he had to do was lay in plans to cut them off when they got there. Those plans would have to wait for tomorrow and first light, though. Hunkering down for the night, he wrapped himself up in his wings. He'd slept in worse places, under worse conditions.

"We move out at first light," he snapped. A sea of bobbing heads around him said the rogues under his command were on board with that plan. Good.

At the end of this particular hunt, there wouldn't be a trace of Ria Morgan left. The Fallen warrior was simply an added bonus.

By the time the sun rose, Ria was about ready to scream.

She'd woken up alone inside the shelter Vkhin had built for her, warm to her toes and tucked up inside his coat. Which meant she'd done nothing but dream of him, because his scent permeated the damned leather. She had his scent on her hair. On her skin.

Worse, she hadn't stopped replaying last night in her head. First he'd given her the orgasm of a lifetime, then he'd hopped inside her head like he'd never heard of boundaries or personal space. He'd been inside her in every possible way, in some kind of freakish emotional vampirism. Because she'd felt him sucking away her emotions. First the pleasure and the shocked surprise that he could make her feel so damn good—and then the fear and anger as she realized he'd intruded in her mind and wasn't getting out anytime soon.

She should have told him their deal was off. He'd broken a big rule, because head-hopping had never been part of their deal. Instead, she was still dutifully following him as he moved double-time towards the wall. He hadn't even acknowledged what had happened between them last night—sexual or otherwise. No, he'd just tossed another damned granola bar at her and ordered her to eat fast because they were moving out.

She glared at his back. He'd taken back his duster. The leather stretched lovingly over those broad, hard shoulders. Beneath the leather, she could see the outline of the blades strapped to his back and he'd have more. He was armed and dangerous.

And she still wanted him.

Hell.

"How much further?" she asked, because why not ask about the nuts-and-bolts facts? Vkhin wasn't going to volunteer any information and she certainly wasn't bringing up last night.

He didn't stop. "Ten, maybe twelve miles."

"Is it all like this?" She indicated the rusted-out car and the other abandoned bits and pieces of human life. People had lived here in the not-so-distant past. Those people were gone now and their cars and houses and things were just leftovers in a wasteland. She couldn't bring herself to care as much as she should have. Shit had happened here, was still happening.

"Pretty much." Those big shoulders shrugged carelessly, his booted feet making short work of a pile of crumbled asphalt.

She knew she couldn't blame what had happened here on the Fallen—humans had managed to screw things up just fine on their own—but the images her drones had shot hadn't told the full story about the sheer scale of the Preserves—the place was far larger than she'd ever dreamed. And it was rotting away, eroding real slowly as nature and the Fallen reshaped the place into something else. She eyed her surroundings again. When she'd trained to run the drones, she'd learned the importance of finding patterns, breaking what she saw down into shapes and parts. No matter how she looked now, though, nothing here was familiar.

"You're not much for talking, are you?" she asked, because she was feeling mean and frustrated.

"I talk." He didn't sound as if he cared, though, and that was part of the problem, wasn't it? She stayed around him much longer and she'd care too much, while he'd just walk away from her double-time and never even realize the damage he'd inflicted. Which sucked. And made her want to torment him just a little.

"Fine," she snapped. "You want to talk about what happened last night."

"Not particularly," he growled.

"Last night, you talked just fine," she said sweetly. "I distinctly recall your saying a whole lot of things, Vkhin. Asking me what I wanted."

He stiffened, but he didn't slow down any. Damned if he didn't speed it up. "I fucked up," he admitted. "You want me to admit it out loud? Fine. There you go. I should have kept my distance and kept my goddamned hands off you."

The hurt feelings came right on back, and she was willing to bet she was going to get even more familiar with them before this hike was over. "Right," she said snidely "Because you hated what you were doing that much."

He stopped abruptly and she plowed straight into his hard back. Classic. She should have seen that move coming, but she'd been blind where he was concerned. No reason why today should work out any differently.

He swung around, catching her upper arms in his hands. Steadying her before she tripped and fell on her ass. His hands clamped down when she tried to wriggle away, however, so maybe he wasn't just playing the gentleman. He glared down at her.

"I liked it too goddamned much, Ria. That's the problem right there. You came and I lost control."

"You got into my head," she agreed. "That was a mistake."

"Yeah." His voice was hoarse. Rough. "But I got out. And it won't happen again."

"Why not?" she had to ask the question because he was driving her crazy and she didn't want to accept the sad fact that he didn't want to kiss her again. Not when she was starting to want so much more from him.

"Because I'm trouble, Ria," he said flatly. "What do you know about the bond?"

"Not much," she admitted. "Just the one favor for one soul part."

"You ever wondered *why* we want those souls, Ria?" His eyes bored into hers. Hard and fierce, he didn't back down from this and she doubted he'd ever back down from a fight in his life. Should have been scared, but one of his hands slid up, finding her cheek. Stroked. She wasn't sure he even knew he was doing that, touching her as if she was someone special and he couldn't bear to lose that connection with her. She wanted to lean into that touch, explore the new sensations he woke in her.

He kept right on talking, not waiting for an answer she didn't have. "I can smell your emotions right now, Ria, and they're goddamned delicious. Arousal. A little sweet trepidation because you know I'm not lying about the danger. You think that's sexy and you're curious about what else I could show you. Don't be," he said, his voice hard and mean. "Don't wonder about me, Ria. When the Fallen were exiled from the Heavens, the archangel in charge took away our wings and then, just for a little added fun and games, he took away our ability to feel anything but the darkest of emotions."

"You can't feel?" Those words of his made no sense. He felt. She knew he did.

"Not the gentler emotions," he said. "Hunger, lust, rage—we got to keep those. But all the good ones? Those are long gone, Ria. I don't do love because I can't, not first-hand. What I can do, though, is feel what you're feeling. I can get my emotional high that way and make no mistake about it. I'm an addict. I crave those feelings and, every single day, I'm jonesing for my next fix because a male can only go so long before the soul thirst overwhelms him. Most of the Fallen, they bond with a human—get their fix that way."

"And if they don't?"

"Then the soul thirst takes over and that Fallen goes rogue. I was too close again last night, Ria. It can't happen again."

"Again."

"I lost control once. I had a bond mate and I took and I took from her. Every single emotion she had, I lapped it up."

"What happened to her?"

He stepped away from her. "What happens to any bond mate if her bonder isn't careful. I took it all. I left nothing for her. She died in my arms, Ria, because I was a fucking, careless beast. So don't romanticize this. I belong right here in the Preserves with every other Fallen angel who couldn't manage his thirst."

She shouldn't have pushed, shouldn't have made him open up to her.

But, oh, God. She's wanted to *know*.

He'd almost given her something last night, wrapped around her in the dark shelter. His intensity had frightened her, and then his intrusion into her mind and soul had been too much.

This was worse.

Maybe, he was the monster he claimed to be. She didn't know if he could be redeemed, didn't claim to be an expert on his kind. All she could do was stare at his back and wonder if she was crazy to hope. To think that maybe they could work something out between them that was more than a rescue and less than a bargain.

As she reached out a hand, the sound of a chopper broke the silence.

CHAPTER SEVEN

Ria wanted to cry, wanted to force Vkhin to admit she'd been right after all. MVD *had* come for her. The police unit's telltale red and white logo branded the bird's tail and the open bay door promised someone was ready to bring her home.

The chopper changed things.

She stopped walking. She was minutes away from rescue.

"See?" She pointed towards the bird chewing up Fallen airspace, even though Vkhin hadn't turned around yet. His gaze went right to the chopper, though, so he'd seen, too. "I told you they'd come for me. I'm going home, Vkhin. Without your help."

"Wait," he said and she wanted to scream. That was rescue up there. She didn't need him, didn't need his diabolical bargains. Of course, maybe he didn't intend to let her scramble aboard.

Suddenly desperate, she darted out into the open and threw an arm over her head, waving madly. Seconds. She only had seconds to get the pilot's attention before the chopper swung round and continued the search pattern somewhere else. She *should* have stayed put, waited for help to come to her.

Behind her, Vkhin cursed roughly and strode toward her. His arm snaked around her waist, dragging her back under the cover of the trees. "Don't," he growled.

"Don't what?" She pushed at the arm restraining her, angry tears stinging her arms. "Don't try and get out of here on my own? Don't make this happen for myself?"

"Don't be stupid, baby." He moved them further back under the canopy, his gaze raking the sky. Taking in the approaching chopper. "You don't know who or what is out there."

"That is my team," she hissed. "That is my unit up there."

"Maybe." His voice was as implacable as the arm he'd wrapped around her waist. "But how do you know this isn't a trap?"

She didn't. But she didn't see any danger, other than the very real possibility the chopper wouldn't see her. Would keep on going and never land for her. She clawed at his arm, desperate to run back out and draw the chopper's attention. Already, the bird's course was arcing, the pilot heading north into a slow, gentle turn as he turned away from her hiding place and back towards the crash site.

No. She opened her mouth to say something and the horizon exploded.

Rogues filled the sky, their wings beating powerfully as they swarmed the chopper.

Gunfire rang out. Those bullets weren't, she thought, sick with fear, going to be enough. There were too many rogues. The chopper's blades stuttered.

Slowed.

"No," she whispered.

The blades stopped and the chopper plummeted towards the ground. Seconds later, the shockwave washed over her and smoke filled the sky.

There wasn't going to be a rescue.

She was still alone here. She couldn't even begin to think about the new loss MVD had just taken. There had been someone in that chopper. Maybe more than one. And now they were gone.

The arm around her waist loosened. Let go. "MVD doesn't know what you know, Ria." His voice was cold and flat. She wanted to turn around and hit him. Scream out the frustration building inside her. "They thought you went down on a recon mission."

"I sent my pictures out." She clung to that fact like a lifeline.

"No." He shook his head and she forced her hands back down by her sides. She wasn't going to give in to the urge. She wouldn't hit him. She wasn't an animal. "I told you, Ria. We blocked that transmission. All MVD knows is that you found something you thought was important. Information you tried to send them, but the transmission broke up."

No one knew.

"Move out," he snapped. "Because, if those rogues saw you—and I'm betting they did— they'll be here in under an hour. You move, or you die."

Ria moved.

He'd expected that. Her would-be rescuers were dead and she still wanted to live. So she let him push her at a brutal pace. He kept an eye on the horizon, though, and there was no missing the small figures chewing up the air.

The rogues were coming.

An hour, tops, and that tail caught up with them and all hell broke loose. He planned to have Ria well over the wall before that happened. He didn't know how he kept the rogues from simply flying over and after her, but he'd figure it out. He had to.

The trees came to an end and they were face to face with the wall.

Vkhin stopped the steady up-and-down and she cartwheeled, trying not to plow into his back. She was too close. Going too fast.

"We're here," she said, even though what she was seeing now required no explanation. The wall had been growing larger and larger, a big bad motherfucker slowly filling up the empty horizon. Three hundred yards away, there was no ignoring what that wall meant.

She was almost home.

The wall was the dividing line between the Preserves and civilization. He didn't understand why so many of his kind had described the wall as a thing of ugliness. That wall was goddamned beautiful in his eyes, because the brick-and-mortar magic of it was going to make sure he did the right thing here. Even if he wanted to, he wasn't following Ria Morgan out of here. He couldn't touch that warded wall for long and he'd be dead before he hit the top.

"Now what? We go over?" He knew he should disabuse her of this idea she wouldn't give up. They weren't getting out together. He wasn't going anywhere.

"You do. I stay here." He strode over to the wall, looking for the rungs set into the smooth surface. He'd give her a leg up, she'd climb, and that would be that. They were out of time. "But first you've got something to give me."

Simple.

The look on her face warned him she wasn't on board with the plan, however. "You can't stay here." Her fingers open and closed by her sides and she didn't move. "That's suicide, Vkhin."

Maybe she hadn't got the memo that he'd been fighting his own battles for millennia. He looked down at his own body and he could see the power there. The weapons bristling from his back and sides. Yeah. He wasn't precisely a helping of helpless, so she shouldn't be worrying about him.

"I can hold my own," he said. Which was an understatement. He didn't plan to leave one of the rogues shadowing them alive. "But, even if I couldn't, I can't go over the wall."

"Can't or won't?"

"Can't." He found the rungs, set deep into the wall. She'd have to stretch a little because the handholds had been placed with a male in mind, but she'd be able to do it. "Come over here and start climbing."

"No." Her feet didn't move, so he headed back towards her. He'd put her on the damned wall himself, but first he had to part her from that vidstick.

"This is where I belong."

"Why?"

"I've killed," he hedged.

"You're a warrior," she countered. "Isn't a body count expected?"

He didn't want to remind her about his dead bond mate or see the truth reflected in her eyes. She looked at him like he was still one of the Heavens' warriors, an anointed savior who could do no wrong—which couldn't have been further from the truth. Before the Fall, the Dominions had been brutal fighters. They'd held the line in the constant battle between good and evil, but at least they had been on the side of good. Now that they were Fallen, he knew *precisely* which side they were on.

The wrong side.

No. He wasn't doing that to her.

Someone had set metal rungs into the wall. With enough upper body strength and lung capacity, any accidental human could climb on out. Those rungs were a primitive back up system, but right now he was grateful for them, because the sky was still clear. No rescue chopper hovered overhead. Maybe, the Fallen got there soon, but daylight was burning and Ria Morgan need out. Now. Before the rogues caught up.

"I can't cross it," he gritted out. "No paranormal can touch that wall. The whole wall is warded—those sigils are one big keep-off-the-grass sign as far as I'm concerned. I touch that wall, I burn."

Her look was *yeah-right*, so he laid the back of his wrist against the glowing surface of the wall. Sure enough, the skin started burning away before her eyes. The pain was a good wake-up call, too, reminding him he needed to get his head back in the game. Stop fantasizing about an impossible future where he and Ria Morgan got it on.

"Stop it," she cried, and for a moment he wondered if she'd got inside his head, knew the thoughts he was thinking.

He pressed harder. "This is just a taste," he said, as if she hadn't spoken. "The longer I touch the wall, the more I burn. No way I make it to the top."

She lunged towards him, pulling his hand away. "You've made your point." Her fingers cupped the back of his hand, supporting his injured wrist as she tilted his arm left and then right. He probably could have handled his big reveal better, because she was looking at his hand if what she saw hurt her. She was a soft touch, he thought.

He needed her to *move*, so he gave her more of the truth. "No, I haven't. You remember what happened to my last bond mate? I killed her."

She chewed on her lower lip. "I thought you couldn't kill your bond mates."

Cold smile. "We're not *supposed* to kill our own mates, no. That's the final line, sweetheart. When one of the Fallen can't control his soul thirst anymore, when he drinks that last little bit, then he's perfectly capable of killing, Ria. He wants to kill. You have any idea what a soul tastes like, pumped full of all that fear and adrenaline? Pure ecstasy," he growled. "Pure addiction."

"You couldn't stop or you wouldn't stop?"

"Either. Neither. When I let her go, she was dead," he said flatly. "I bonded with her. My help with a favor she needed—in exchange for a taste of her soul. Well, I took a hell of a lot more than that, Ria. I took it *all*. For any other Fallen, that would have been a death sentence." She shakes her head mutely. "Yeah." He watched her carefully. "We do police our own. Once a Fallen gives in to the soul thirst, once he goes rogue, we hunt that rogue down like a rabid dog and we make sure he doesn't hurt anyone else."

"You're still here," she pointed out. "Your two and two aren't adding up here, Vkhin. Either you didn't kill her, or you did and you got away with it. Which is it?"

He eyed her, but she clearly had to have the whole story. Wanted to hear his shame at the reprieve he'd been handed. "Zer needed me. We had a deal—once he'd got the whole leadership situation under control, he'd take care of me."

Zer hadn't been ready or willing to take on the leadership of the Fallen. He'd wanted an assist and Vkhin had provided it. On that one condition.

Zer had found his soul mate and stepped up to the plate, heading up the Fallen like he'd been born to play the part. That made it payback time.

Ria watched him like she knew exactly what he was thinking. "Kill you."

Those memories had tormented him for decades and laying them down would be a relief. Here in the Preserves he didn't need to hide that dark side of himself any longer. Here, he could admit he was no better than an animal and go about the business of dying or holding out until the soul thirst destroyed every last vestige of his sanity. He was almost done here.

"I have every intention of paying that price," he assured her.

Her anger surprised him. "Well, your death wish is going to have to wait, isn't it?"

Not for long. "You, however, don't belong here," he growled. "So you hand over the vidstick and I'll give you a leg up and you can start climbing now."

She looked like she wanted to say something else, but then, thank God, she shut the hell up and came over to the wall. "When I get to the top," she said stubbornly. "Once I see it's clear, then I'll give you the vidstick."

He nodded, even though she undoubtedly was entertaining foolish thoughts of double-crossing him. Elsewhere, there were watchtowers and human military, but not here. And he didn't have time to take her further up the wall in search of her own kind.

"Get up, get over and start walking," he ordered. "Don't stray from the wall. You'll set off the sensors when you cross but, if no one comes out here a second time for you, another ten miles and you should hit a tower. They'll get you back to M City."

"And then what?"

He shrugged as if he didn't care. "You get on with your life, Ria. You want to keep sending out your little drones, you do that. But my job here ends when you hand over the vidstick and cross that wall."

Before she could argue further, he cupped his hands to give her a leg up. She hesitated, then stepped into his hands and reached for the first rung.

And screamed.

Christ almighty, she screamed. Panting, he caught her body as she arched away from the wall, pressing her hands against her body.

"What. The. Hell," he roared.

"Vkhin," she whimpered. "That hurt. You didn't warn me it would hurt."

Her palms were smoking, the skin there cherry red. Like *his*. Before his head could process the intel his eyes were sending, she reached for the rungs again. As soon as her palm slapped against the metal, the smoking started right back up again.

He ripped her away from the wall, peeling her hands off the rungs. Fuck. This was all wrong.

She backed away from the wall double-time, staring down at her injured hands as she sat down, hard, on the ground. "Why can't I touch the wall, Vkhin?"

"I don't know." He pulled off his t-shirt and crouched down next to her, tearing the white cotton into strips and wrapping them around her reddened palms. Not a hygienic choice, but his only one right now. His mind raced, examining and discarding possibilities. There was only one, of course.

"You're not human," he said. "At least, not entirely."

"Excuse me." Her hands jerked in his and he held on tight. "I am one hundred percent human. You think I wouldn't know if I had a paranormal parent? My father was a crotchety old bastard," she said, "but he was human. So was my mother. Find another theory."

"No." He shook his head. "If you were one hundred percent human, you'd be able to climb that wall, baby. Somewhere, somehow, you got a little piece of us." He didn't like where his thoughts were taking him. Three of his brothers had found soul mates—and those women had been human women, with a genetic kicker. Their ancestors had all come from a lost tribe of Israel and who had a mutated strand of DNA.

"How well do you know your family tree?" he asked. "Because, I'm betting, if you go back far enough, you're going to find a female in there who has Israeli roots and whose history got so lost in a diaspora millennia ago that you don't really know where she came from. That she was born to the thirteenth tribe of Israel and marked for us by an archangel."

She eyed him, eyed the wall. The sky overhead was still too damned empty, so eventually she got back to looking at him. "Let's say, just for the sake of argument, that all that's true. What does it mean?"

"It means," he said, "that the archangel Michael tagged your people millennia ago as mates for mine."

Ria Morgan was a soul mate. This was something he'd never considered. Sure, she was beautiful and he'd wanted her from day one, but that just meant he had eyes in his head and knew how to use them. He'd never believed in any of the predestined mate crap the archangel Michael had spouted, but he'd seen Zer, after the male had found his soul mate and that was a thing of beauty. Those two felt something for each other, something Vkhin knew he didn't understand and could never have. That bond wasn't just sexual and it was sure as hell complicated.

It took no-holds barred opening up—*love*—for a Fallen angel to get his wings back. Vkhin wasn't sure he was capable of that. Strike that. He knew he wasn't and hadn't been for centuries and possibly even longer. Still, just the thought of Ria Morgan finding *that* with another male had him growling and that was bad. She was off-limits. He was the transportation, nothing more.

Except that he was the only Fallen on the scene and Ria Morgan needed an out, now. If he bonded with her and she was a soul mate, their bond would give him back his wings. If he had wings, he could fly her over the wall. Keep her safe. Take her *home*.

Was it even possible?

"So?" She glared at him and he figured he'd better make the explanations fast. They were out of time and she was out of patience. Not that he blamed her. Finding out she wasn't completely human had to be a shock.

"So, when the archangel Michael tossed our asses out of the Heavens three millennia ago, he tossed in a redemption clause, too. Michael swore that he'd give each one of us a special mate, a female of worth who could redeem her male." Explaining wasn't his best idea, but there was no way to force her to do this thing. She wanted words— he'd give her words.

"You want me to believe in destiny." Her expression said it all, didn't it? That wasn't the ecstatic smile of a lottery winner that she was wearing. "That someone's been waiting three thousand years for me to come along? Comparatively speaking, Vkhin, I might have been born yesterday, but I'm not that stupid. No one has ever wanted me like that. I'm not some predestined mate for a Fallen angel. None of that is even remotely possible. Your damned wall has probably malfunctioned. That, or you got it wrong and no one—human or paranormal—can cross over it. Which means, we're stuck waiting here for rescue."

She *was* special. He'd known that from the first moment he'd felt her watching him. He wasn't handling this right, but that was no surprise. He was a fighter, not a damned poet.

"We have another choice. I want you," he growled. "We both know that."

Of course, he wasn't going to bring soul mates up in conversation with her. He wasn't stupid. She was already too wary and he'd made his dislike of the bond damned clear. So, if he changed his tune too fast here, she'd be on to him. And this was too important to fuck up.

"Bond with me."

"No." Clearly, she didn't have to think twice and that just proved his point, didn't it. She dropped her pack on the ground and followed it down.

"I'm not asking," he said. "I'm telling." Of course, the bond wouldn't happen if she didn't agree, but he didn't have time to tap dance around this. The rogues would be catching up all too soon, and he didn't see another way out.

"Really." She crossed her arms over her chest and glared at him. "That was perfectly obvious, thank you. You told me you don't do bonds. You said, no way in hell."

Unfortunately, her memory was working just fine. He crouched down on the ground next to her, slapping his hands down around her. "Look up," he growled. "You see anything *friendly* flying around up there?"

Her head tilted back, looking straight up. "Not a thing, Vkhin."

"Right." He leaned into her, but she didn't budge, so he ended up chest to chest with her. "All that clear blue means you and me? We're royally fucked, baby. There's no chopper up there right now, MVD or the Fallen. We've got nothing—except a pack of rogues who are going to show up here anytime now and then all hell breaks loose. You need to get out of here now and, for that, you need me."

She looked at him like she wanted him to be different. Like he'd somehow disappointed her. He told himself that didn't matter. He was doing what had to be done to get her out of here.

"This is all about your deal, isn't it?" She shoved him away and he went. He figured he'd made his point and she'd get with the program quickly enough. Ria Morgan was one of the smartest women he'd ever met, even if she didn't know it.

"Yeah. This doesn't have to suck, Ria. Trust me," he said, feeling the biggest bastard around. His kind seduced and they both knew it. He didn't have to tell her the forever part of being a soul mate—that was a little secret he could take with him right to the grave.

"Bond with me, Ria Morgan."

"This doesn't bother you at all, does it?" She waved a hand at the blades. "Killing. Being on the run. This is just another job for you."

His eyes watched her, but she knew he was aware of their surroundings, too. Anyone, anything came out of those trees, he was ready.

"That's what I am," he said calmly. "You knew that, Ria. And I made no bones about it. I've been fighting for millennia. It's who I am. I kill."

Just the thought made her queasy. How could anyone live like that, day after day? For *centuries*? Fear had her stomach knotted up right now.

"It's not who I am," she admitted.

"Of course not."

The anger was a welcome change. "I'm scared, Vkhin. Scared all the time. I can 't do this, can't live like this. Going up in that chopper, I thought I was being so damned brave. That maybe I'd finally conquered all this fear I had inside me. Earn a little respect. Instead, here I am, stuck inside a prison and we're arguing over who is going to rescue me because I can't do it for myself."

He muttered a curse. "Who told you that you weren't brave?" he asked finally.

"Some things don't need telling." She shrugged. "My dad. The trainers at MVD. Lieutenant Reece." When Vkhin raised an eyebrow questioningly, she added, "The woman who had to push my ass out of that chopper because I couldn't jump on my own."

He stared at her and she got the sense he'd rather be anywhere. Taking on a pack of rogues he understood. This conversation thing? Not so much. "It's okay for you to be scared," he said carefully. "Point is, you got out of that plane. If you couldn't do it for yourself, you made the arrangements to get someone else to take care of business for you. That's just smart."

"You're never scared."

"Baby," he growled. "I don't feel emotion like that. Not since the Fall. Feeling scared isn't something I can do."

"But you don't like this, don't like being forced to bond with me."

"You're different," he said and she wanted to believe him. She searched his face, looking for something, anything, because all her instincts were screaming that this wasn't a male who didn't feel. He didn't wear those emotions on his sleeve, but they were there, buried deep beneath the surface.

"Let me help you," he said. "Let me get you out of here. Maybe, MVD gets their act together and they send another chopper after you. Maybe, that new bird gets here before the rogues catch up with us. That happens, they come for you and they make it, I'll bow out and you can go home with them."

"You don't think that's happening anytime soon."

"No." Clearly, he wasn't going to bullshit her. "I think that if MVD was capable of hosting a successful rescue mission, that first chopper wouldn't have gone down. Plus, MVD would have been waiting here for you. They'd have been watching for movement at the wall, would have sent in one of those UAVs you pilot for them. They didn't do that. They sent a rescue team and that team went down."

"What happens?"

"If we bond?" He stood up and eyeballed their surroundings. "We have sex." Yeah, he definitely wasn't going to sugar-coat this. "I ask you to name your favor. You do that. Then we have ourselves a connection. I can sense your emotions, feed off of them, and whatever favor you ask for gets taken care of. In this case," he hesitated, "I think I'll get my wings back."

"Since I'm a soul mate?"

"Yeah. So," his eyes bored into hers, "Question is, will you do it?"

She shouldn't. Making a bargain with a Fallen angel was about the most unsafe choice she could make. He was a killer. Ruthless and hard and unfathomably older than she was. Worse, he'd just said he pretty much wasn't capable of feeling anything.

So why was she so certain he was a good man? An honorable soldier. He'd keep his promises because his sense of right and wrong was unbending. Vkhin's world was all black and white—he didn't do grey, even though he lived in a world of shadows. God, that was sexy. And he deserved more, so much more. He hadn't wanted her *before*. Hell, she had only a passing acquaintance with telling the truth. She'd lie and cheat and steal to get her job done because, at the end of the day, she was going to do her part to keep the human residents of M City safe.

And to keep Vkhin safe, too, because she didn't want to watch him die and she didn't want to leave him behind here. "Yes."

"Then we go over there," he said, indicating a tumble-down building tucked close to the wall. Maybe, before the Fallen had taken over here, that building had been a hunting lodge. Maybe, it had been part of the princely estates that had dotted the Russian landscape for the last thousand years. Now, the building had decayed, was a mere shadow of what it had been. Russia was a sybaritic empire that had eaten itself up and collapsed when the underdogs had finally risen up and demanded their own day and their own turn at fucking things up royally. All that was left here were ghosts and whispers of power-that-had-been and that was just too fucking perfect.

She'd fall there.

CHAPTER EIGHT

Taking her indoors was the gentlemanly thing to do, but Vkhin hadn't been a gentleman. Ever. He'd been bred to be a fighter. A cold-hearted, cold-blooded killer whose only redeeming grace was that he fought for the Heavens. Remaining outside was more defensible. Outside and you didn't end up trapped beneath four walls and a roof when they came for you.

But, damn it, he was going to do this right.

Even if he only had a half hour tops.

He kicked aside what was left of the door and shouldered his way inside. The lodge was full of dust and antiques, the bones of former splendor. And a huge bed. That bed could have held two Russian empresses and half their court and it worked just fine for him. The cover was almost gone from age so he tossed his duster over the top. Would have to do. Didn't matter how much he wanted more for her. This was all he had to offer tonight.

He just hoped to hell it would be enough

"You bond with me," he said, wrapping his hands around those slender fingers exploring his face, "you won't ever forget it. You give me those words, let me in, and you're going to see the marks on your skin every single morning that we're bonded. You ready for that?"

"You're talking about the bonding marks."

She'd have seen the tattoo-like markings in MVD's files and on the images her drones had shot. Those marks were black bands around the wrists of both the human and the Fallen angel. Patterns varied, as did the thickness of the markings, but every single Fallen-human pair was marked like that. The greater the favor, the darker the markings. Like a really big *paid* sticker or a cosmic receipt.

"Does it hurt?" She toed off her sneakers, reaching for the zipper on the jumpsuit. With her hair tangled around her face, she looked impossibly sexy. The loud rasp of the zipper coming down took his gaze with it. The jumpsuit parted, revealing a pale vee of creamy skin and the lilac tease of her bra. She bent over, pushing the heavy material down her legs and that simple movement had his blood pounding in his ears as he drank in the erotic sight of those long, slim legs and the cheeks of her ass cupped by the thin cotton of her panties.

Something inside him came alive, reacting fiercely to the thought of her in pain, being hurt.

"No." His fingers clenched on the gold bracelet in his pocket. He should give it back to her, but he wanted that piece of her. The fragile links had been next to her skin, warmed by her skin. Carried her scent even as they'd been caught and torn and broken in the chopper crash.

She wasn't going to end up broken like that bracelet. He'd done everything he could to keep her safe, both from the rogues hunting them in the Preserves and from himself. He couldn't be trusted. He knew that, even if she didn't. It was why Zer, the leader of the Fallen, had agreed to let him be the one to come here. To hunt *her*. Get in, get her pics.

If he bonded with her and she was, as he suspected, his soul mate, their bonding would restore his wings. The only way out of the Preserves was up and over, so that math was simple. He'd do what it took.

He'd take her. Hold her. *Have* her. And, if he couldn't control himself, couldn't control his demon side and the soul thirst, he'd kill her. Just like his last bond mate. It was a chance he had to take, he reminded himself, because she'd die if the rogues got their hands on her.

But at his hands would be worse.

She trusted him.

Barefoot, she moved towards the bed, then hesitated. Reaching down inside one of the pockets on the leg of her jumpsuit, she took out the vidstick.

"Here," she said. "You take this for now. Keep it safe for me, okay?"

The plastic case was warm from her skin. His fingers closed over it. He could destroy it. Could leave her here to face the rogues or simply snap her neck, if he was feeling charitable. That knowledge was in her eyes.

"Okay," he answered and wondered what exactly he was promising her. Because this was becoming more than a simple exchange of favors. He knew that. Hoped like hell she did, too.

He tucked the vidstick in a side pocket of his pants as her knees hit the side of the bed and she turned. He was close. He inhaled deeply, dragging the scent of her skin deep inside him. She smelled of the smoke from their fire and the outdoors, and beneath that, woman.

Because that attraction and trust was not going to be enough. Not against a Fallen angel determined to bind her body and soul. He'd tell her what to do, give her commands. He'd do it because he was going to keep her safe and get her home, but she'd still resent his orders. And she wouldn't have a choice. Once they'd bonded, she'd be *his*.

This first time was going to have to be quick, too. For her, he wanted to be the lover she needed, but time was a luxury they didn't have.

"You're all mine now," he said. He'd seen firsthand the sensual games some of his fellow Fallen played. Dom and sub. Erotic games. His Ria was too independent for those kinds of games and they were out of time. Not now. Maybe not ever. She didn't take orders.

But she would now. He was going to make sure of that.

He was going to touch her.

Hell, she was going to touch him. Never mind that this was a really bad idea.

He was all big, tough warrior as he came towards her, as if she was a battle he needed to win. Heat shot through her as she watched him come. He pulled off his shirt with quick, efficient movements and she fought the urge to move towards him. God, he was beautiful. His body was big and hard, the sharp planes of his stomach where the golden skin disappeared beneath the waistband of his pants drew her eye. He was disciplined. Honed by battles she couldn't begin to imagine. And the thick erection pressing against the front of his pants reassured her. She wasn't alone in this unfamiliar maelstrom of desire. Vkhin was there, with her.

"Come here," she whispered, stretching her arms up towards him.

His head turned away from her for a moment, eying the empty fireplace on the other side of the room. "I wish," he began and then stopped. "I can't make a fire for you," he said fiercely. "The smoke would give us away immediately and we need all the time we can buy, but I don't want you to be cold."

"I'm okay," she said and she was. She was nervous and aroused, but she wouldn't be afraid, she told herself. They were being hunted, but Vkhin would never allow anyone to hurt her. She wanted to take care of herself, even if the danger made her a bundle of nerves, but she appreciated the extra security. Loved how feminine and cherished it made her feel. She'd never felt cherished. As if someone wanted to take care of her not because she needed it but because he wanted to do that for her. A gift.

"Lay back." His guttural command had her panties dampening. "Do it," he ordered when she hesitated.

She did as he ordered, the sound of her body shifting on his leather jacket unbearably loud in the stillness of the room. When he got closer, she could smell the smoke and sage scent of the man, clean and hard and undeniable.

Need blazed through her. This was going to work. Everything was going to be all right. Maybe, they'd get through this and everything would be fine. Maybe, she wouldn't walk away from his bed with a broken heart.

He came down over her. Not touching her yet, just caging her between the bed he'd made for her and his body. Those broad shoulders blocked out the room.

"We don't have much time, do we?" she asked because she wanted him naked, but she understood that wasn't going to happen.

"No," he agreed softly. One powerful forearm came down beside her head. There was a flash of metal as he set a knife to one side where he could palm the blade quickly. "We don't. But I'm going to make this good for you," he promised.

He didn't need to make her that vow. She knew this would be good with him. She wanted him, wanted him inside her so she could take him deep and hard and make this part of him hers. Their relationship would be a temporary thing, just long enough to get them over the wall and back to M City, so she pushed that regret out of her head. She'd have him now and that was going to have to be enough.

"No," she countered, reaching up for him. "I'm going to make this good for you."

"Make?" His eyes flared and he leaned down into her. "No one makes me do anything, baby. Not for millennia."

"Too bad," she challenged, because she wasn't going to let him dominate her. Not here, not in their temporary bed. If she did, she sensed she'd lose him. She'd meet him face-to-face, as equals. Whatever he gave, she'd give. "Right now, I'm thinking you're all mine."

She slid a hand down his chest. His skin jumped beneath her touch, but his eyes never left her face. He just froze, like an animal facing the unknown. "You're going to like this," she whispered. "I promise. Okay?"

Heat flared between them, as sensations slammed into her, and, oh God, she wasn't cold any more. Her hand wrapped around him through his pants. That hard length pressed into her flesh and she wanted more. Finding his zipper, she got it open and then there was nothing between her palm and him. Just the slick, heated length of him sliding against her skin.

Anticipation swept through her. He'd fought battles. He'd killed to do the right thing. And now he held himself above her, motionless. Waiting for her touch, her command. So she reached out to him. Just one curious stroke of her finger, sliding down that slick length. Soft and gentle, she explored him, teasing the soft, vulnerable skin. No rhythm. She just touched where she wanted, where he was unfamiliar. Soft and slow. Pleasure filled her, a powerful sense of connection.

"Let me," she whispered. She wasn't sure what she was asking for. Permission to touch, to take. For him to lower those barriers he kept up against the world. Spreading her fingers, she stroked around him, expanding her horizons. Letting him fill her up.

What she got was pleasure surging through her as he groaned, shoving that part of him against her hand. Demanding more.

Leaning up, she licked his nipple. The erection in her hand thickened, lengthening. His sexy growl warned her he was done playing, but she couldn't lose this connection with him. All she had was this handful of stolen minutes and she wanted every one of those seconds.

"I'm not done with you." Would she ever be done? She could feel the tension building in him, warning her that he was fighting for control and that it wouldn't take much to send him over the edge. His hands tangled in her hair, holding her tight. His mouth brushed against her hair, his thumb stroking her cheek.

She got her hand wrapped around him more tightly and squeezed gently, a long, luscious movement that took her hand from the tip to the base. She wanted to cover every inch of him, stroke until he was pushing himself into her palm, coming in fast, hard strokes. She'd fantasized about having him like that, watching him while he came just for her.

"That's enough," he growled. His head came down, his mouth covering hers. Hard and dominant, his wicked kiss stole her breath away. He tasted of sage and male, of something wild and untamed and impossibly addictive. She'd been kissed before, but none of those other lovers came close to measuring up. She'd never forget this first real taste of him, his fingers fisting in her hair as he stroked his tongue inside her mouth, that part of him warning her what was coming next.

Thank God.

His lips parted her, opening her up further for his exploration. His tongue drove inside her mouth again. And each stroke drover her higher, until all she could think of was this male holding her. Kissing her.

"Vkhin," she whispered.

Pulling away from his mouth, she slid down beneath him before he could stop her. The hand she'd wrapped around his erection squeezed gently and found his zipper. His hips bucked as she slid his pants out of the way, shoving his erection into her hand just like she fantasized. Harder. Silently demanding more. Good. She wanted all of him, wanted to taste this part of him as well. Her clit was swollen and hard and she wanted to ride him, rub herself against him, because he could make her feel so good.

"I want to taste you," she warned. Above her, he groaned and she drank in the dark sound. She wanted to explore all the dark pieces and parts. Learn him inside and out. For now, though, she sucked just the tip of him into her mouth and held him there. Heated and wet, her tongue explored the lush underside, teasing the nerves hidden beneath the flared head.

He muttered an indistinct curse and she looked up, sliding her mouth down his erection again. The connection slammed into her.

He yanked her up, ripping off her panties as he parted her thighs. She was wet and open and aching.

"I'm touching you," he warned. "How brave are you now?"

"God, please." She couldn't take much more of this, didn't want to wait when all they had was this handful of stolen minutes. She couldn't keep him, had to let him go back to the world where he belonged but, right now, he was all *hers*. Every raw, demanding inch of him was *hers*. She slid her fingers along the heated length of him, wanting him to feel like she was feeling. Needy and urgent. Empty.

His fingers, blunt and hard, parted the saturated folds of her pussy. Just the tips. Just like before. "God, more, Vkhin." She rocked forward, sliding herself against his fingers. Pleasure speared through her. "Give me more."

"Yes," he growled.

The large blunt tip of him was at her needy opening. Pushing in. Hard. Heated. Determined. His fingers petted her clit, desperately. Making her wetter, making her ease for him.

He pushed slowly inside her and, God, she took him. Sweet, feminine heat surrounded him, her slick passage clenching down on him. "Bond with me."

"Yes," she growled. "I'll bond with you." He pressed forward, sinking deeper into her and she arched up into his hold.

"Ask for your favor," he growled. He nipped at her lower lip with his teeth. Marking her as if he couldn't help himself and he wanted her to know she belonged to him. Was hungry for *her*.

Something flashed in his eyes, but her arms were reaching up, locking around his neck and pulling him towards her. "Get my pictures out," she said. "Get my pictures out. I want that vidstick on my desk in M City."

He froze, his body stilling. "You should be careful what you ask for, baby."

He drove into her again, cupping her ass in his hands so he could lift her up, find that sweet, hidden spot inside her. "Done."

He drove himself deeper and harder into her, pushing them both towards the edge as his hands tightened on hers, her fingers curling around his. Rode the final explosion of pleasure as the orgasm tore them both, the bonding marks spiraling into existence around their wrist with each heated clench, thick black strokes of ink telling the whole world that he and she had themselves a deal.

Vkhin got up and off Ria, dropping a quick, hard kiss onto her forehead as he got dressed. He wasn't facing this bare-assed, not with the army they had coming after them. He regretted the need to get going, but things weren't going to slow down just because he wanted more time to hold her.

She followed his lead, dressing rapidly, and his regret grew as she covered up her skin. He wanted to spend hours touching and kissing her skin, learning her, but he was out of time for the first time in millennia. "You think it worked?" she asked.

As the first shock wave of pain slammed into him, he knew had his answer. He was Changing and, yeah, it was going to suck. He passed her the shotgun so she'd have something between her and any rogue who got to the party early. "Anyone comes through that door, you shoot first. Ask questions later."

His skin crawled, his nerves howling in revolt. Yeah, it had worked. He wasn't surprised. He'd known what he felt for her. He loved her and he wanted those wings for her.

Still, he hadn't been prepared for the magnitude of the pain. He was going down for the count, no way around it, and if the rogues caught up with them before he finished here, the fight wouldn't end well for either of them.

Christ. The word hissed out from between his lips, more prayer than curse as he staggered, bracing his hand first on the wall and then on his knee. The pain bent him over and proceeded to tap dance on his nerves.

Maybe he should have been all poetry at being handed the possibility of a dream, but this wasn't going to be pretty. He didn't know the exact mechanics, but he'd seen the vid. Hard and rough, the Change took a Fallen apart from the inside out and reassembled him. He just hoped it was fast, because trouble was closing in on them even faster.

The unmistakable sound of something large and heavy struck the roof overhead. The roof held. Temporarily. Even she had to see that their shelter couldn't withstand that kind of strike for long. Sure enough, the blow repeated and a shower of dust and debris rained down on them, accompanied by the sharp crack of too-old wood splitting.

"They've found us." She pointed the gun at the ceiling, then back at the door. As if she wasn't sure which direction trouble would come from.

"Keep that gun up," he gritted out through his teeth when she lowered the weapon at the sound of his groan.

She ignored his instructions. "You're hurting." She pushed against his side, taking his weight as he staggered from the second blast of pain radiating through him.

Another heavy blow shook their refuge. *God. Damn. It.*

His lips peeled back with a snarl. "Gun. Up." She didn't go unprotected.

She braced him, braced the gun. "I've got it," she snarled right back.

Pride flooded him. God, she was fierce and that was a beautiful thing. *She* was beautiful, inside and out. He'd wanted this because he wanted to get her out of here. More than a promise to a bond mate. He needed to do this for her and he would. Whatever it took, he got her over that wall and back home.

He sucked air in desperately as a third wave of pain hit. Head down, teeth bared, he panted through the agony. The skin on his back tightened, the white ropes of scars where Michael had ripped away his wings forced open as the new wings began pushing through the old skin, reaching for the surface.

Faster.

Each rough inhale brought with it the familiar, unwelcome scent. The metallic tang of the rogues. Coming for Ria. "We have to get out of here," he bit out. "The rogues are coming, Ria. We need to be ready for them. Don't let them pin you down inside."

She smoothed a hand over his shoulder. That gentle touch undid him. "You can't go anywhere, Vkhin." He didn't have to see to know she had that stubborn look in her eyes. She'd made up her mind, picked her course. "This is insane. You're hurting."

He was, but pain had never kept him from doing what he had to do. He wasn't failing now, not when Ria's life was at stake.

"Go," he growled, leaning heavily on her until she stumbled towards the door. Another heavy blow shook the building and she staggered, fighting to keep on her feet.

"Serve you right if I shoot you," she grumbled.

He took a step forward and the tip of his new wings slammed through his back, tearing through the scarred skin of his back. Each violent wrench split him a little further open, until he threw back his head, gritting his teeth. The bones of his shoulders and ribs broke and reformed, flowing into an alien shape. He couldn't, wouldn't, scream when the enemy was so close but the rush of sensations was too fast and hard. Everything was coming back to him. He'd been prepared for the pain, but not for the emotions.

Sliding the safety back on, Ria dropped to the dusty floor beside him. "You don't have to do this alone," she said. He'd planned to, though. He'd been determined to do this alone. He didn't know how the Change worked, but having her here, with him, felt right. It sure as hell felt better. Her hands pulled his head down into her lap, one stroking his forehead, the other palming his gun. Anyone came through that door, she had the leverage she needed to blow their goddamned heads off.

He'd never been proud of anyone before, not since the Fall. Now, he was proud of Ria Morgan. She'd been thrown into his dark and violent world and she was holding her head up. Holding her own. He wanted to tell her that he loved her, but the pain was coming back now, faster and harder than before and all he could do was hold on.

Her voice was whispering something to him and he wished he could hear the words, but pain was a red tide washing over him. Instead, he pressed his face against her leg, savoring the soft, vulnerable warmth of her thigh beneath his cheek. Sucking a breath in, he rode out the pain as her scent hit him hard. This was for her.

This was so right.

Bone cracked loudly, the sharp sound ricocheting off the walls of their decaying refuge. This was it. He focused on everything he felt for his Ria, because he had to keep her safe and this was the only way to do it.

His wings erupted through the passage they'd carved in his back.

"Oh, my God, Vkhin." Her thigh tensed beneath him, shock pushing through her. "You did it."

The pain receded and he lifted his head. Twelve feet long, his wings covered the floor, lush, dark feathers covering the finely curved arches. He felt stronger than before, the weakness draining from him as suddenly as it had hit. He stretched, savoring the pull of his muscles. His wings weren't there for pretty. They were weapons.

Muscled strength designed to send him driving through the open sky after his prey, to make him bigger, stronger. Faster. He opened them hard and fast, because now he had what he needed to get her out of here. Loss and savage, fierce gladness filled him. Now he could keep her safe—so he could lose her again.

Pushing rapidly to his feet, he furled his wings tight against his body, let the feathers disappear back into his skin. If she looked, he knew she'd see the dark outline of his wings tattooed against his back, waiting for the moment he summoned them.

The roof shook, hairline fractures appearing in the plastered ceiling. He held out a hand to her. "Come on."

She didn't hesitate, gave him her hand and let him pull her to her feet.

"Alright," she said. "Where are we going?"

"Out," he said. The need to take care of her burned through him. "It's time to go home.."

CHAPTER NINE

Shit hit the fan before Vkhin even cleared the lodge door. There was no time to fly out as the rogues came in hard, palming weapons and rushing their exit point. Ria looked up, because maybe she believed there was still a chance backup came riding to the rescue, but the sky was blue—and empty. Still not a chopper in sight, so she and Vkhin were clearly on their own here.

The full court press meant Vkhin wasn't getting his wings open to take her up and out, either. There just wasn't enough room to spread those wings of his. No, the rogues just keep moving forward, trying to pin them or drive them back inside the building. She had a bad feeling about that option.

"You ready for this?" Vkhin didn't look at her, but his whole body screamed anticipation. A fight was coming and he just couldn't wait. She opened her mouth to answer—although she didn't know what to tell him—but then grabbed his shoulder as dust kicked up beneath a pair of powerful wings downstroking their way onto the battlefield.

The rogue who landed between them and the pack was just more bad news. He was as large and as dark as his soldiers, but anger and rage had twisted his features into a dark mimicry of the beautiful angel he must once have been. He drew in his crimson wings as he landed, the snap of the membranes closing sharply final. Those wings were the color of blood, the sharp warning crimson of a shepherd's moon.

That one was clearly the most insane of a bad lot.

"Fallen." The rogue's voice sounded like splintered wood, rough and broken. She didn't want to know what kind of shit life had handed out to make him sound that way.

Vkhin's cold eyes burned into the other angel. "Hazor. Leave us."

"Can't do that. It's too late for this one." Hazor flicked a finger at Ria. "She shouldn't have come here, shouldn't have poked her nose in our business."

"And?" Vkhin sounded icy, bored.

"Hand her over, Fallen. You do that, you go right on your way. My fight isn't with you." The pack crowded closer behind their leader, their faces twisted with avarice and rage as they stared past Vkhin and right at her. God. This wasn't going to end well.

One of the rogues slipped closer, his wings trailing on the ground. "She's pretty, Hazor."

"Tasty," the third hissed.

"And she has something of ours," Hazor pointed out. "So you tell me, Fallen, if we're doing this the easy way."

"Easy for who?" she asked, slipping her hand around the gun's handle. She knew bullets alone wouldn't be enough to save her here, but the cool metal was comforting. A potent reminder that she could do something here, even if that something didn't work.

Hazor ignored her, speaking directly to Vkhin as if she didn't exist. Didn't matter. "Give us the female and the vidstick. That's all we need and we'll be off."

She wondered for a long moment if Vkhin could, would make that trade. Would he have, if they hadn't bonded? The delicate black markings twining around her wrists confirmed his commitment, but she didn't want to sit back and watch. Not this time.

"I can't do that." Vkhin's blades came out as he refused the other's offer and his wings unfurled from the tattoo on his back. Ready to fight. Ready to uphold his end of their bargain.

The rogue angel shook his head mockingly. "Can't or won't, mate?"

His companion sneered. "Look at his wrists. Look at hers. They've bonded. They're soul mates." Whispers filled the air like rain hitting leaves. Sibilant. Shocked.

"What does that mean?" she muttered. "Soul mate?"

Vkhin's hand tucked her behind him. "Don't move. I'm going to kill them and then I'm going to take you home."

He was keeping secrets from her. It was far too late to start second-guessing herself. She'd made a decision to trust him when she'd decided to lay down next to him and do a little bonding of her own.

Hazor was more than happy to clue her in. "Soul mate means you're his one and only, darling. You're the needle in the haystack the archangel put here on this Earth for your mate to find. He finds you, he gets himself a free pass. The little matter of his Fall? All forgiven and forgotten and he gets himself back his wings."

Those dark wings of his flowed around her, long, lethal curves with deceptively soft feathers. Was she just a means to an end for Vkhin? He was ruthless. But was he that heartless?

Vkhin didn't move. "She's more than just a pair of wings."

So fuck it. She took a step forward, putting herself alongside him. She wouldn't hide behind him. Either she stood next to him—or she didn't.

Hazor smiled slowly. "If she's a bloody soul mate, we'll just have to kill you first, Fallen."

Hazor and his pack died today. Vkhin ignored the rage pounding through his veins because anger got a warrior killed on the battlefield more times than not. That fury was still there, though, beating at him as he eyed his oncoming. His bond with Ria Morgan was something special. He wouldn't let them defile it.

Inhale. Exhale.

Find the ice cold center in his heart where he was all lethal killer. He planted his boots, rocking back on his heels as readied himself for the attack. When her arm brushed against his, though, the rage threatened to come right back up from the hole where he'd shoved it. *No one threatened his female.*

He'd kill these and have enough time to get her over the wall. With the wings, that was possible. Quick weapons check said he was good for the moment. He had blades strapped to his forearms and thighs, plus a handful of throwing stars. And the shotgun in its scabbard on his back.

He'd start with the shotgun.

Beside him, Ria had her chin up, facing forward. Determination was written all over her beautiful, stubborn face.

"You need to know something," he said. Bracing the stock against his shoulder, he sighted down the barrel and took aim. Fired. One down.

"You're packing enough ammo to take them all down?" she said hopefully.

"Two things." No time to reload, so he pulled and threw, the first of his blades arcing through the air with deadly intent. "First, since we're soul mates, you don't die until or unless I do." While his target hit the ground, he pumped the gun hard, the spent shell finding ground as the next up hit the empty chamber.

"You just now got around to mentioning that?" She squeezed off a round and got one of her own.

"You can still hurt," he said grimly. "Don't underestimate how much you can feel."

"Got it," she snapped. "What's second on your list?"

"This," he said. Raising her hand to his mouth, he launched a throwing star. Four down. "I love you. Now stay the hell back."

The pack surged and he sprang into action

Pull. Cut. Fire. He cut ruthlessly through Hazor's pack. Feet apart, boots planted, he was a cold whirlwind of death. He'd been trained as a Heavenly warrior—and then exiled. He'd spent three thousand years street fighting and no one was getting to his soul mate. Not now. Not ever. That mate stood shoulder to shoulder with him because she was done hiding and there was no safe ground here anyhow. Still, he got his body between her and their oncoming, ignoring her protesting growl.

He pumped and fired, the shotgun taking off the head of the rogue nearest them in a crimson spray. There were still too many rogues on their feet and circling.

"Reload," Vkhin snapped, tossing the gun over his shoulder. "Now, Ria."

Her hands grabbed for the barrel. "On it."

Hazor headed his way, the bastard clearly done watching from the sidelines as his pack took hit after hit.

Vkhin didn't hesitate. Going on the offensive, he strode towards Hazor, his boots eating up the ground. As he closed in, he got one hand wrapped around the handle of his blade, pulling the sharp edge in close to his chest. Hazor wouldn't hand him his opportunity, so he'd take it. The blade was just another extension of his hand. Part of him. All he had to do was hit his target.

Hazor struck first, driving across the downed bodies of his pack. Fyreblade out and reaching for Vkhin's throat. Vkhin feinted, letting the blade cut through newly empty air. As Hazor's body followed the fyreblade, Vkhin drove his own blade up with lethal force. A quick prick and penetration that unerringly found the soft spot between the other male's ribs.

Vkhin's other fist rose and fell, striking with lethal force. He didn't need a blade to inflict damage. His fist drove in and out, battering his opponent. There was nothing elegant or pretty about a blade fight. The air around them smelled of shit as the blade bit deep into the other's lower intestine.

Score one for him.

Driving forward, he took back the ground. Step by step. Until he and Hazor were skin-to-skin, hand to hand. Arms locked and fighting for control of the blades. Hazor's blade slashed across Vkhin's forearm, a long, shallow burn of a cut, and Vkhin cursed.

Hazor's blade came back around again, as the rogue Fallen's lips peeled back. "I'm going to skin you inch by inch, Fallen. Flay those bonding marks right off you."

Vkhin struck hard and fast with his free hand and Hazor's head snapped backwards with a satisfying crunch. He followed with a fast series of blows. Punch. Strike with the blade. His fist plowed into the other's face, then planted the blade deep in the exposed neck as Hazor's head followed the blow. One hard twist of his arm and the other's head listed.

"Not today," he said through gritted teeth. His blade took Hazor's head. *Not ever.*

As Hazor's body hit the ground, the final rogue picked himself up off the ground and swung towards them. Vkhin reached for weapons—mind already calculating whether it would be quicker to pull the blade out of Hazor's neck or palm the back-up blade strapped to his thigh—but Ria already had it.

As he'd fought, he'd been aware that she'd been laying down protective cover to keep the remaining rogues from massing. Now, the shotgun came down over his shoulder. He braced himself, holding steady.

"Ready?" she growled.

"Always," he murmured.

She fired, the shotgun driving down into his shoulder as the butt recoiled. There was a roar of heated sound in his ear and then the last rogue went down and stayed down.

"Ria." Vkhin's dark voice spoke Ria's name like her name was a promise.

She looked at him. Looked away from the carnage surrounding them. Fighting wasn't pretty. War wasn't, but sometimes, there were things that had to be done. She'd done exactly that, so she'd be okay. She realized she was rubbing her arms with her hands and forced herself to drop her hands by her side. She was going to be okay.

Really.

"We need to go," he said. He held out his hand to her. "Come here, baby. We're going to get you home now."

"How?" Suspicion colored her voice. "Neither of us can touch that wall."

"No." He shook his head patiently, unfolding his wings. The dark arches stretched up into the sky behind him. "That's why we're going to fly."

"You want me to fly. No way." She took a step backwards, but he kept right on holding out his hand—that big, strong warm hand. This close, there was no missing the black swirls of their bonding marks, a tangible promise. Right now, Vkhin belonged to her, was hers in every way possible until he'd given her that one favor. That was how the bond worked. One promised favor. One bond—until the favor was met. Despite the raw heat in his eyes that promised he'd give her everything, he'd leave when he'd fulfilled the terms of their bargain.

"No flying, Vkhin." There. Her words sounded confident, sure. He'd get the message and together they'd figure out another way out of here. Given the carnage surrounding them, it might even be possible to wait it out until a search party found them.

Because there was no way she flew. The wall cutting them off from the rest of the world was too tall, too high. That wall stretched upwards hundreds of feet and she'd done thousands in the chopper, but the chopper had crashed, hadn't it? She sucked air in, her chest painfully tight. Her mind knew the air was coming in, but her lungs didn't seem to have the message. Each new breath was a struggle. Heat flushed her face, warming her body unbearably.

"Ria," he crooned. He took a step towards her, closing the distance. His arms came around her and the gesture was too tender. That searing intimacy wasn't what she'd expected from her brutal warrior. There was tenderness in that touch, even if he didn't know it. "Breath, baby."

"I don't fly." She didn't let her doubts color her voice.

"You flew in here," he pointed out calmly.

"And that was a mistake. One I don't intend to make again."

His hand reached up and stroked her cheek. "You know there's no other way out."

"Find one." She could be stubborn when she needed to be.

"Why?" he asked. When she didn't answer right away, he kept right on pushing. "Why don't you like flying?"

She stared at him mutely.

He gave that her patient look, the one that did unspeakable things to her insides because she'd never expected to see patience on his face. Worse, he dropped a kiss on her forehead, as if he'd known her for years and they were the kind of couple who had years of anniversaries under their belt.

"You need to tell me, baby. We have to go over the wall, because there's no other way out. That's the way the Preserves work. You fly in. You fly out." His head turned away from her, looking up. "The Fallen will be on their way, but I don't know when they'll get here. Maybe, your people will come for you, too, but these aren't certainties. Do you need to take that chance?"

He wasn't forcing her. He was *asking*. He took his watchdog gaze off the still-empty skies and eyed her face instead, as if he thought he'd find answers there. Maybe he'd find an answer she didn't have, because she didn't know why she hated flying. Just that letting her feet leave the ground like that, watching all that empty space open up between herself and safety, wasn't something she took lightly. She wasn't sure, however she could explain to him what she didn't fully understand herself.

She dragged in one breath, then another, while he just held her, waiting for her to make up her mind.

"I love you," he continued. "You want to stay here until MVD or the Fallen come up with a chopper, we can do that." The understanding in his voice almost broke her. "Maybe, we hike up until we hit a watch tower and see if we can signal for help."

"It's not a good idea, is it? But it's not as if my last flight ended well," she pointed out. She wanted him to tell her she was wrong, but she already knew he wouldn't.

"Safest course of action is to go now. These rogues aren't a threat," he dismissed the remains of their attackers with brutal practicality. "But there will be more."

"Soon?"

He shrugged, but he didn't drop his arms. She gave in to temptation and laid her head on his chest. That heart beat of his was strong and steady. "Probably. So you tell me what you need to do. You need to wait, we wait. I'll take care of anyone who comes after us," he promised. "You'll go home, one way or another. I promise you that. Trust me."

God. She did, she realized. She trusted him.

"Alright." She tilted her head back, watching his face. "Then let's go now. I'm ready to go home, Vkhin. Take me there."

When he wrapped his arms around her, she tensed, her heart beat hitting train wreck speed. "Your feet are still on the ground, baby," he whispered.

His wings unfolded, slid free from the dark tattoo inked across his back, dark and powerful. As strong and hard as the male they bore up. The soft rustle filled the space between them.

"This flight will be different," he promised. "No more crash landings, Ria."

"Yes," she whispered and those wings opened completely and beat, hard and strong, driving them away from the ground and up into the sky.

He kissed her as he took her up, sweet and slow and deep. She held on to him, losing herself in the man and the indescribable heat of his mouth. The sensations of soaring and weightlessness.

God, he was incredible.

Too soon, her feet bumped against the balcony of her flat. A quick flick of his wrist had her balcony doors open and then he was backing her inside.

CHAPTER TEN

The need to get that damned vidstick to her desk drove him forward. He needed to wind up this damned favor business, so he could get on with the important things. Like figuring out a way to keep his soul mate forever. In his arms. Where he wanted—needed—her to be. He wanted her to choose him, choose them, and that meant holding up his end of their bargain so she wasn't bound to him.

He didn't know what he would do if she didn't choose him.

Pushing the thought from his head, he forced his fingers to pull the slim stick out of his pocket. Part of him really didn't want to let go because what he had with her right now was still so much better than the emptiness of before that he almost didn't want to take the chance of losing.

This was going to be her choice.

Since she hadn't specified *which* desk she wanted the pics delivered to, and he was choosing that much. That, he smiled slowly, was a mistake. Her bedroom worked just fine for him. The vidstick landed on her desk with a small click and he turned around to face her.

"You've got your pictures," he said. "On your desk. Just as you asked."

Her eyes widened and the bond between them snapped. Just like that, the direct in he had on her emotions was gone. It was okay, he told himself. He could still sense her, still had the bigger connection because she was still his soul mate and there was nothing that could break that greater bond. He didn't need to drink her emotions because he had emotions of his own now. Too many emotions. Love, tenderness, *fear*—all cascading through him and making him stand there and stare at her because he didn't know where or how to start.

Judgment time.

Except... he still needed to call in and make the situation clear to the other Fallen. Snagging the charging cell from her desk, he made a quick call to the Fallen. The what-the-hells and the details covered five minutes and, when he snapped the phone shut, clean-up was already headed for the Preserves. He'd take the pictures in later. Ria hadn't considered the longer term implications of her request; he'd delivered the vidstick to her desk, sure, but the moment the device had hit the surface, he'd been free of his promise. Sometimes, being Fallen was all about the letter of the law and not the spirit.

"You're going to take the pics." She didn't sound upset, but, now that the bond between them had snapped, he wasn't sure how she felt anymore. And he was going to do the right thing, he warned himself fiercely, and stay the hell out of her head. He wasn't coming in, not until or unless she invited him. God, he wished he didn't have that need to do the right thing burning at him, because he was desperate to know what she was feeling.

He looked down at his wrists. He'd done her favor and that superficial bond between them had snapped. The black ink of the bonding marks was retreating, disappearing, despite the other connection that was still there. He wondered if she felt it, too, or if was just him. He didn't know. Maybe, he'd ask his brothers. Maybe, that was too personal and just maybe every male took to the soul bond differently. He didn't. Hell, he didn't care—all he cared about was standing there on the carpet too far away, watching him. All these new emotions left him raw and open.

The black ink on her wrists faded, disappearing back into her skin. And he still didn't know what to say to her. Yeah, he needed to take those pictures back to his base, hand them over to Zer and the others to check out. Those pictures had the potential to be explosive and securing them was a priority. He should have said all that but, instead, here he was, just staring at that pale, bare expanse of skin and wondering if she missed the bonding marks. At all.

He should have got inside her head when he had the chance and maybe he would have learned how to please her, give her what she needed.

"It's okay," she said, scrubbing at her face with her hand. Her feet stayed planted, though. She didn't move from that spot she'd picked out on the rug, but her eyes ran over his face. He wished he knew what she was looking for. "You need to take the pictures back to the rest of the Fallen, I get that. I'm not sure MVD would know what to do with them, anyhow. Probably some sort of knee jerk reaction like dropping a bomb on the Preserves."

"Wouldn't be such a bad thing," he finally volunteered, when the silence had stretched out too long between them. If, of course, the bombs actually did their thing and killed what they hit. If all that happened was that the wall came down, well, that was a road he didn't want to go down.

"Maybe." She shrugged. "But maybe there's someone else worth saving there. Or trapped." A shadow passed over her eyes. "Like Lieutenant Reece."

He didn't want to tell her that the good lieutenant was either dead or wishing she was. The next words out of his mouth surprised himself. "I'll go back," he said gruffly. "Look for her, if you want."

Her face just watched him, tear-filled and sad. "We should recon first." She wrapped her arms around her middle. "Send in a drone. Because if she's really dead, there's no point in risking anyone else, is there?"

She'd barely known the lieutenant, but she had the other woman's back. She had his. She didn't leave anyone behind and that was just one of the reasons he loved her. And, even if he hadn't had reasons, he suspected he would have loved Ria Morgan. There was something about her, some indefinable, inescapable quality that made her *her*—and conquering him heart and soul, the way she had the rest of him.

The empty space between them seemed like an impossible

gulf, a carpet-covered emptiness he shouldn't cross. She might not be one hundred percent human, but he wasn't human at all. She deserved better than a used-up, too old angel who'd been evicted from the Heavens for all the right reasons.

On the other hand, he thought, as his booted foot took a step forward, fuck it. He'd already broken every rule there was, so why follow the rule book now?

"I love you," he said, then said the words again because those words felt right.

Not just because she was his soul mate, the woman fate had hand-picked for him, but because he'd loved her before he'd known what she was. She was his other half, his missing half. When he had her wrapped up in his arms, close to his heart, he knew better than to let go. Ever. What he felt for her, with her, was so much more than the fiery heat, the pleasure building between them. Touching her, tasting her, was more pleasure than he'd ever had in his life, but the connection he felt with her went so much deeper.

He was hers, body and soul.

He existed for her, to keep her safe, to make her dreams and her fantasies come true. And for the quiet moments, when he could hold her and she him and just breathe in the familiar scent of her. After millennia without emotion, love was an unfamiliar, fascinating, wonderful storm that had taken him by surprise but that he wouldn't give up. With or without his wings, he was all hers and he was holding on to the incredible woman he'd found.

Forever.

Ria's feet were moving before she could second-guess herself, eating up that empty piece of space between them.

She met him halfway, her arms coming up, sliding over his broad shoulders and pulling him close. No more space. Just the two of them, as close as they could get.

The bond was gone. Her wrists were bare and she was free. Common sense said she should send him away and count her blessings. She'd made a bargain with one of the Fallen and the price hadn't cost her soul. She knew others weren't so lucky.

She'd been warned.

But she still wanted this one Fallen angel. Vkhin was *hers* and she wasn't giving him up.

"Stay," she said and he nodded, his arms tightening around her.

"You want to give me a reason," he growled, "or am I flying blind here?"

She placed her hand over his heart, savoring the strong, steady beat.

"The bond's gone," she whispered. The marks were gone, true, but she still felt him. Her body craved his, yearned for his touch. She knew what it was to explore that big, hard body, to lose herself in the pleasure he offered.

And to find something, *someone*, in all that heat. Vkhin. What she felt for him hadn't disappeared with the bonding marks. She needed more than just a favor from him, wanted more than a bond mate's relationship with him.

"That's one," he agreed.

"I love you." She gave him back his words. She wanted to share this part of herself with him, tell him what she'd never told another male. He was hers and she loved him. Bond or no bond, they belonged together.

"And I love you," he promised, his head lowering to hers.

He wrapped an arm around her waist and pulled her close. The jumpsuit parted easily when he got a thumb on the zipper and tugged. Revealing her inch by inch. That sure, deliberate touch sent pleasure spiking through her. He wanted her, saw only her. And she was wet and aching for his touch.

She wanted him to taste her.

All of her.

Wanted him to lay her down on the bed and taste every secret place, find the magic they'd shared in the Preserves and recreate it all again.

"You're staying with me," he growled and it was more satisfied statement than demand. "Now. Tomorrow. *Always*."

She leaned her head back against the arm holding her up, just watching. There were no favors here. No rules. She wanted to leave, he wouldn't stop her. If she wanted out from his arms, all she had to do was take one little step to her left and she'd be free and clear.

"Always," she agreed, sliding her hand up his arm. He looked like he wanted to say something more, but she didn't want to talk any more. All she wanted was to taste.

He threaded his fingers through her hair, and closed the last few inches of space between their mouths. The arm around her tightened, brought her impossibly close. Stroking a thumb over the small of his back, she stole a moment to savor the heat, the hardness of the male holding her, through the fabric.

His lips against hers were a simple little tease, a gentle brush of his skin on hers. The kiss was a slow and sweet game, but sensation rocketed through her with that first touch of his mouth against her skin.

Mine.

His head came up. "We've still got the soul bond, Ria." Her name was an intimate promise on his lips. "This time, it's forever. For as long as you want me."

She felt his mouth against her ear. "Vkhin," she gasped. "You think I can afford a soul bond?" Here with him, now, she felt alive and unafraid, as if she had wings herself and could use them.

"This one's free," he promised. "A gift from me to you. You want me, you have me."

"Yes," she whispered, her fingers marching up his chest. "Forever."

That new bond pulled them close to each other. Something more. Something *right*. He was right there, waiting for her to recognize him. To let him in. His arms closed around her, pulling her close.

Finally back where she belonged.

And check out *His Dark Bond*, available now from Kensington!

HE HUNGERS FOR HER BODY...

Zer is no angel—well, not anymore. He's explored every flavor of sin imaginable, drinking in the pleasures of humanity. But now he must find the woman who carries his salvation in her very blood... a woman like Nessa St. James.

AND HER SOUL

Nessa has considered the bargain the Fallen offer. Anything she wants in exchange for accepting Zer's bond? No way. Not her. Not when she finds out about the mind-blowing ritual involved, and the marks of surrender that will ink her skin. But with a serial killer to stop and centuries of experience on his side, this is one job Zer's going to nail.

ABOUT THE AUTHOR

After ten years of graduate school and too many degrees, **Anne Marsh** escaped to become a technical writer. When not planted firmly in front of the laptop translating Engineering into English, Anne enjoys gardening, running (even if it's just to the 7-11 for Slurpees), and reading books curled up with her kids. The best part of writing romance, however, is finally being able to answer the question: "So… what do you do with a PhD in Slavic languages and literatures?" She lives in Northern California with her husband, two kids and five cats. You can visit her online at www.herfallenangel.com.

Made in the USA
Lexington, KY
05 April 2014